Aphrodite's Sister:
The Goddess of Emotion
Book 1

Published by Goulden Publishing
www.GouldenPublishing.com

Dedication

This book is dedicated to my mother: your love and enthusiasm are what started this book. And to my editor, Alissa: your executive decisions and thoughtfulness are what finished it. Thank you.

Table of Contents

Chapter 1

The Amendment

With a huge grin, I swung the door open and stepped into the house. *Home*. I had forgotten what it felt like to be here after being away at school for such a long time. A familiar warmth overcame me as soon as I stepped through the doorway, instantly reminding me of my childhood.

"Mom? Dad?" I yelled. I heard no answer. So I called again. Again, no answer, which was unlike them. My parents were always home and ready to greet their children returning from training. Maybe there was some sort of celebration I hadn't heard about—though that was unlikely, since *all* Gods and Goddesses were summoned for any celebration in the Heavens.

"Petra!" My mother's voice called, laced with pure horror. "Call Timothy!"

I followed her shrill to a corner in the atrium. There my father lay sprawled on the floor holding his leg in agony. Protruding through his shin was what looked like a stick, or the shaft of an arrow. My parents 'feelings attacked my senses violently, like an atomic bomb exploding in my body in one sudden vibration.

"Mom? What happened?"

Breathlessly, she said, "Your brother was angry."

No other words were necessary. I called Timothy with the press of a button on our wall transmitter, and then quickly rushed to my parents 'side. I thought I might scream, but I did not—I felt nothing, though I knew I should have. Something must have happened to John, something awful.

When Timothy arrived no more than two seconds later, I stood and headed for the front door. I felt my mother wanting to call for me, so I turned back to her. The look I gave her must have left no question as to where I was headed, for she came over to me, giving me a glare that was simultaneously terrifying and pleading. With my eyes, I asked for her permission to go after my brother.

I kissed her forehead and whispered in her ear, "I will fix this," and then went out the door, my father's screams echoing behind me.

∞

I found him near a California sea cliff off the coast of Point Dume. Angry gusts of wind and haunting black clouds swirled around and above us. He seemed to be deep in thought, deciding whether to jump or not.

I had two choices—tackle him off the cliff, giving Poseidon permission to punish us both, or do the harder, more agonizing thing and talk to him, try to reason with him, and maybe find out what was going on inside his head.

"What the Hades were you thinking, John?"

I tried to make my voice sharp to penetrate the wind. He took one step closer to the edge, as if tempting me. I sighed and moved closer, watching my footing on the rocky precipice. I took another step, and then the wave hit me and I staggered back, throwing my hands up to shield myself. When I regained my footing, I looked down and found that I was not wet. I threw my head up, expecting to see that the tide had crashed over the rocky cliff face. But it was not a wave of water I had felt but a wave of emotion—John's. He was crying. I hadn't noticed before because his long, golden bangs covered his face, and he stood with his back to me.

Is he crying because of what he did to father?

As I moved toward him, the waves slammed into me over and over, crashing against the front of my body. When I got close enough, I realized I'd been wrong about the reason for his tears. They were not tears for what he had done to father, but for what a Goddess had done to him.

"You have got to be kidding me!" I yelled, but then bit my tongue, quickly regretting speaking my thoughts aloud.

My brother spun halfway around, agitated. "What?"

I yelled, trying to get my words to him before another gust came and carried them away. "John, please! Tell me what happened!"

"H-How do you know?" He shook his head angrily, brows creasing above his golden eyes.

"Those don't feel like tears of remorse," I yelled, "but of a broken heart." I tried whispering my last words, giving the wind permission to scatter them, but they reached him anyway.

John fell to his knees, his face in his hands, and began sobbing uncontrollably.

Damn the wind.

I shook my head and rushed to him, skipping, almost floating over each jagged rock. I knelt behind him and gently placed one hand on his back—I could feel emotions better when touching. Therefore, I could feel his pain and loss more sharply. She left him.

I grabbed his shoulder, turning him to face me, and swallowed his body up, cradling him in my arms.

"It happened to you, too, didn't it?" I asked.

The story of Eros 'legacy had been told for thousands of years. The son of Aphrodite was a God who had angelic wings, carried a bow, and shot golden arrows that caused anything with a soul to fall in love with the first thing it saw. Over the centuries, things have changed. In our time, we no longer use golden arrows but music—a specific tune or song played for the intended lovers. Nor is the God of Love called Eros anymore, but John Ambrosi.

According to legend, Eros once fell in love with a mortal named Psyche. She was said to have been one of the most beautiful mortals on Earth—and Aphrodite despised her for it. So she sent Eros to Earth to make Psyche fall in love with a beast. But when Eros entered Psyche's room and saw her sleeping, he observed how beautiful she truly was. Distracted, he accidentally nicked himself with his own arrow and fell immediately in love. Realizing he could never perform the duty his mother had given him, he carried Psyche away to his palace in the Heavens, where he treated her to the best luxuries.

For years, Eros hid himself from her, afraid she would not love him once she found out who he was. But one night while Eros slept, Psyche snuck into his room and shone a light over him, revealing his true identity. After that, he never saw her again. Some stories say he let her leave, for he felt betrayed. Some say Aphrodite took her away. And some say she fled to the Underworld. But every story concluded with Psyche leaving Eros a broken God, shackled by his love for her.

After her departure, Eros promised himself he would never fall in love again, for love only brought pain. So he cursed his own arrows. If anyone were to be pricked by one of them, they would feel only the torment he was destined to feel forever.

How could this happen again? Is it the God of Love's fate for his beloved to leave? Who is this Goddess, and for what reason did she abandon my brother? Whoever she was, she was long gone. I could sense that from his tears.

Still cradling my brother, I began to fall into a trance, remembering when my eldest sister, Eva, had suffered a broken heart. I remembered each day perfectly, like it was me who had traveled through her versions of the Underworld and Paradise. Unfortunately, there were more days in the Underworld. It felt like a permanent stay during which every grotesque, disturbed, and deceased soul there tore her down more. I had felt everything through her then, and I'd hated it. Hated my gift. True hell was unleashed in me as she experienced heartbreak, for I felt everything with her. I developed a new kind of anger in having to feel her suffering and promised, just like Eros, that if that was what love was like, I would never want it. I never again wanted to experience those feelings.

A century later, I continue to keep my promise to myself. Love annoyed me. It was a torturous chain that thrashed at the hearts of its victims. I could still sense my sister, sick and angry, lying on the ground crying as if she had been stabbed in the chest a dozen times.

As I held my brother, my clothes grew heavier, soaked from the rain and his tears. I barely noticed that the storm had reached us, and it was now pouring. I extracted his face from his hands and looked down into his golden, bloodshot eyes with all the compassion I could muster.

"I am still here. . . if that even means anything anymore." He gave me a slight nod, and I smiled.

"Let's go home."

Only time could heal what John had done to my father. Father had only been trying to calm him in the midst of his heartbreak, but John's rage was blinding. Although they were not to be used, every God of Love still carried the golden arrows. They had been passed down through each descendant— from God of Love to God of Love. My brother had grabbed one of the cursed things and stabbed it into my father's leg.

When my mother recounted the story, she became angry and flustered all over again, reliving the moment. I stared back at her blankly, trying to stop myself from feeling her feelings.

They are not my own.

My family and I were very grateful for Timothy. He was the descendant of Asclepius, blessed with the gifts of medicine and healing. If the poison had reached Father's heart, Eros 'torment would have been permanent, driving my father—or any God—insane. But Timothy had arrived just in time to stop the poison from spreading, leaving Father with only a disgusting scar and a partially mortal leg. Thankfully, Father had not lost his sense of humor.

After supper one evening a couple of weeks after the incident, I decided to go outside and relax on our porch. I immediately felt at ease while admiring the Heavens' sunset. It was beautiful, and unlike any sunset on Earth. I sat back, allowing the colors to swallow me whole and shine all

around me. It was as if I were sitting on the edge of the horizon—or at the edge of outer space.

I looked down, through the Heavens' transparent ground, and saw the colors entwine with the puffy white clouds beneath my feet. I breathed in deeply, inhaling the sweet scent of peaches from the orchards in our front yard. Peaches were my favorite thing about home. I smiled at the thought and continued inhaling and exhaling, big deep breaths, completely relaxing my whole body with each exhale.

Suddenly a tiny, tense hand gripped my shoulder. I turned around to find my mother looking down at me with wide eyes.

"Mom?"

"Sorry, Petra . . ." Her face was beautiful, glowing.

Each time I looked at my mother, I found it hard to believe we were related. We looked nothing alike. She was petite and delicately put together. In contrast to my wavy blonde hair and blue eyes, her bronze, easy-flowing hair was combed but not styled, lying flat on her head. She had golden eyes, just like my brother and sister, which always glowed brighter when something was wrong. They were glowing like a full moon as she settled herself next to me.

"Are you okay?"

After what happened with Father, things were not the same as they used to be, but it had been slowly getting better. I could feel, however, that my mother was holding in something heavy.

"So…no more Gaianus?" she asked at last, referring to my school.

"No." I laughed. "I left my training there, and I plan to begin at

Titanus."

She eyed me warily, her eyes still glowing brightly.

"Gaianus is not challenging enough for me. They were teaching us how to live *with* mortals. Did you know that?"

"Yes, Petra, that is why we sent you there and not to Titanus."

I leaned back to get a better look at her face. Suddenly, I did not want to hear anything else she had to say.

She knew? Does Father know, too?

"Mom, perhaps I'm not understanding correctly, but is it your wish that I live with mortals? Are you trying to kick me out of the house?" I joked.

She sighed. "Honey, you *need* this." She put her hand on my knee, allowing me to feel her concern—as if I could not feel her already. I pulled away. I didn't understand.

"But what do I *need* from the humans?"

I wanted to run from this conversation, so I started to stand up.

"Petra," my mother said sternly, grabbing both my knees this time, sitting me back down next to her. She stared into me with her solemn eyes. "It is *essential* that every God, Goddess, every single immortal should understand what it's like to live among mortals. You will learn more than you think, and you will become full with a wisdom that will humble your *soul*.
That, Petra, is what makes the best and most powerful immortals in all the Heavens."

I sat still, having nothing to say. We settled into a long silence.

"Honey, do you know where the constellation Libra is?"

I gawked at her, half smiling. "Yes, of course, Mom. It's between the constellations Virgo and Scorpius."

"Yes! Do you know why the Libra lies in the middle between the Virgo and the Scorpius?"

I shook my head. "I didn't know there was any significance."

A small, pleasant smile took over her face. "Honey, everything has significance. See, Petra, the Libra is the symbol of the scales." I gawked at her again. *I knew that.* "And the Virgo is the Earth sign of the Virgin." *Knew that too.*" And the Scorpius is the water sign of the Scorpion." *A given.*

"For us, the Virgin represents the power of the mortals—innocent, naïve, harmless—and of Earth itself. And the mortals have always portrayed the Heavens as being as impenetrable as the sea. And then we have the story of Orion…"

I shook my head, not remembering the story.

"Oh, Petra." She leaned back and tilted her head, clearly disappointed. "It is where the Scorpius came from. Apollo felt threatened by Orion and had Hera send down a giant scorpion with impenetrable armor to sting him until he was dead." She stopped to see if I recalled the story yet. I shook my head slowly.

"The Scorpius became an emblem of the Deities, given to us by the mortals, and the scorpion's stinger represents our power. The scorpion knows only how to protect *itself*—like us, it is impenetrable, strong, a predator. Every immortal is like this. That is why there was so much betrayal, infidelity, and war during Cronus 'reign."

"And Zeus 'reign," I muttered.

She gave me a sideways glance. She'd never liked me discussing politics. "Yes, but everyone knows Zeus went to Earth to exchange knowledge with the mortals, which Cronus would never do. Zeus hoped we could have balance in the Heavens like the mortals attempt to have on Earth. It was by living beside the mortals that we learned of balance, and that we should not try to be stronger than what is absolutely necessary.

"The weighing scales represent our hope to have this balance in both realms—on Earth and in the Heavens. However, our power is too great to find this balance alone. We need the humility of the mortals to help achieve it, and once we all learn how to do so on Earth, we will then be able to have it in the Heavens. To help us remember that we need this balance, Zeus placed the Libra in the stars right next to the. . ."

"*Virgo and Scorpius,*" I said with her, understanding fully now. I sat motionless, looking at her wise, smiling eyes.

"Wow, Mom," I paused. "Great story. So what will you have me do then?"

She seemed about to say something but then stopped, as if thinking how to word it properly. I was curious as to what solution she would suggest. "Your father and I," she began, and paused. "We want to send you to a school down on Earth . . . to an all-mortal school."

And there it was. That was what she wanted from me. I searched my mind for something I could use to argue against her, any angle I could bring to the table. After mentally sifting through the points I could try to use in my favor, I slowly started to grasp the fact that I had been beaten. All my reasons not to attend school with the mortals seemed stupid and unrealistic now, and would make me look like a child if I were to bring them up.

I sat back against the porch wall in defeat. "Well, where do you want me to go then?" I asked with a sigh.

"Colorado," she said, smiling.

Chapter 2

The Omen

The bright Montana sun shone through my truck's windshield and into my eyes. I lay in the driver's seat—bundled up, feet pressed against the passenger-side window panel and legs tangled in the blanket wrapped around me.

As my eyes adjusted, I realized that I had been dreaming. I was not in Montana at Titanus. In front of me was a large sign that read "Regis University." I sighed.

That's right, I'm in Colorado.

I stared out the window, past the sign, to the snow-capped mountains— too beautiful to be real. After stretching for a long time, I finally opened my door and hopped out of the truck with a thud. My breath instantly froze in the frigid air when I exhaled. I knew it had to be below zero, but I didn't feel the chill even though all I had on was a simple white T-shirt and jeans. Nevertheless, I went back in my truck, grabbed my jean jacket and backpack, and put both on.

Before leaving, I checked myself in the mirror, attempting to coax the long, blonde strips of hair into their usual spots. Giving up, I turned around with a deep sigh to face the new adventure ahead.

I walked around the side of the student center, where the open commons led up to the main building on campus. The building was breathtaking, three stories tall and over fifty yards wide. Its center was reminiscent of a house—a simple granite and brick base with a triangular façade at the top. On the façade was a white cross. The entire building, and those to the side, was the color of sandstone. On either side of center was an elongated row of windows, topped by a light blue mansard roof.

As soon as I became enveloped in the crowd of students and professors, I began to sense their thoughts and feelings around me. They were quite loud at first, making me feel like I was in a wind tunnel, with gusts of emotion blowing at me constantly. But I had learned in my training at Gaianus that if I focused on one person at a time, I would only feel that person. So I began to do this, and most of what I sensed was shyness, confusion, and fear. It felt weird and unsteady.

I began to focus on the students looking at me. Some were curious, and some intimidated. *Do I look intimidating?* I looked down at myself—at my small, pasty hands; my too-skinny arms and waist; my thin, stick-like legs; and, lastly, my disproportionately small feet. *Nope. Not intimidating...not even in the slightest.*

The campus was not huge, yet not tiny. I reached into my backpack and took out my schedule and map to see where I would be heading for my first class. As I turned down a pathway, I sensed someone following me. Trying not to be too obvious, I turned my head slightly to see who it was.

Maybe another Deity?

A girl brushed quickly past me, shoving my left shoulder hard and knocking me forward, causing me to drop all the papers I held in my hands. I gasped and shook my head, thinking maybe I should start getting used to that kind of treatment.

The girl must have realized how rude she had been—or she forgot something—because she stopped walking. I watched out of the corner of my eye to see what she was going to do next. She pivoted and paused, then slowly made her way back to me wearing an honest and apologetic smile.

She had tan skin and blonde and brown highlighted hair tied back in a curly ponytail. I felt my eye twitch—either from the sun glinting off her teeth or from what she was wearing. I didn't know whether to be amazed or shocked.

Around her neck was a Montana Grizzlies lanyard. A baggy silver and maroon Montana hoodie sagged over her black spandex pants, which also sported a Grizzlies logo on the bottom. She was a walking billboard—geared up head to toe with University of Montana sportswear. I looked up to the sky, toward my ever-so-regal parents and the Elders. What were the odds that the first person I would run into—literally—would be a walking advertisement for the one place I so desired to be?

The symbolic message taunted me. I should have been angry, but the girl stopped in front of me and bent down, her curly ponytail falling in her face as she grabbed for some of my papers.

"I am *so* sorry," she said, still wearing that innocent smile.

I tried not to look at her. I felt like the Gods were laughing at me—a sign of mockery. Or some kind of sign.

"No, it's fine," I mumbled curtly, still not looking at her as I raced to gather all my papers. I lifted my gaze to her for just a second, saw her staring at me, and quickly shot my eyes away. I stood up in a hurry, and so did she— about half a second behind me. She met my eyes again. They were beautiful. Were they green, or blue, or...yellow? I couldn't tell.

I gave her one last nod before quickly walking past her and toward my class. Before entering the classroom, I looked back to see if Montana was following me, but all I could see of her was the Grizzlies backpack bobbing up and down as she headed in the opposite direction.

I shook my head slowly and muttered, "That was *so* weird."

Chapter 3

Jessica Eris

By the third class, I was getting tired, and began to fall asleep as the professor wrapped up his lecture. I leaned forward to prop myself up on the desk, thinking it was closer than it actually was. My elbow slipped, and my body fell forward, causing me to almost hit my head on the desk. Quickly, I looked around to see if anyone had seen. Several people were staring, and a few were starting to snicker.

I knew I was supposed to feel stupid or embarrassed, but I didn't feel anything. All I could do was read my classmates 'faces and sense what *they* felt . . . and what they were feeling *for me* was embarrassment.

I looked at the row behind me, at the few who were still laughing quietly, and I saw her—Montana. Of course. Another sign from the Gods: laughing at me.

She looked at me, and then immediately leaned back in her seat and whispered something to the brown-haired girl sitting behind her. The girl must have whispered something encouraging back, because Montana got up from her desk and made her way to mine.

I looked quickly down, hoping she would go away.

"Hey!"

My disappearing act apparently didn't work, so I picked my head up slowly. My eyes immediately fixed onto hers—I was determined to pinpoint their color this time.

"Hey," I replied in a low voice.

"I saw you in the hallway earlier. I ran into you by accident...?" I couldn't figure out if that was a statement or a question. "Yeah, I remember," I muttered.

"Yeah, well, sorry again 'bout that. So my friend over there told me you just transferred here?"

I turned to look at the brown-haired girl. She looked right back at me, grinning. "Uh, yeah," I said slowly.

How did she know that?

"Where from?"

Instantly, my mind began working desperately. I had not prepared myself for such a simple question—for any questions, for that matter. I had no plan to make friends or talk to anyone. To mortals, my school didn't exist, so I decided just to keep it vague.

"From Texas," I said confidently. *Texas? Where the hell did that come from?*

"Oh, cool. You're from Texas?"

I wanted to tell her no, but that would just lead to another question requiring another answer. "I just went to school there. You're from Montana?" I asked, in an attempt to steer the conversation away from me.

She looked at me, surprised. I nodded to her sweatshirt. She looked down, then back up at me, and smiled. She had a beautiful smile.

"Yeah, I'm from there," she said still smiling. "So anyways, my friend and I were wondering if you wanted to play on our soccer team here at school."

"Yeah?" I mumbled. "Thanks, but I think I'll pass." I gave her a polite smile.

She had been leaning on my desk, but now stood up suddenly as if the desktop had burned her hands. "Alright, that's cool. We have a meeting this Wednesday if you end up changing your mind. . ."

She must be the captain, promoting her team as she was—either that, or the team was just that desperate for players. I looked back at the brown-haired girl. There was something about her. Something different. She sat comfortably in her desk facing me, still grinning widely.
I wonder…

For a second, I'd forgot Montana was there.

"Yeah, sure. Thanks," I said, nodding my head while still observing the brown-haired girl. I looked up and gave Montana one last smile. She remained standing there for a while, staring at me in silence, before finally moving back to her desk.

Thank the mocking Gods that's over. I just wanted to get back to my truck and end this day.

Thankfully, class ended, and all the kids hurried out the door—too quickly for me to notice I was the last one left in the room. I had just exited the classroom when someone nudged me from behind.

"Hey, Petra."

I turned quickly and saw it was Montana's friend—the brown-haired girl.

"Hey?"

She grabbed me, and within a flash, we were back in the classroom. She pushed me into a desk, and I collapsed onto the seat.

"Didn't think you were the only one here, did you?" she said with a smile.

I cocked my head and squinted. "No, guess not."

She sat herself on my desk. Her glowing, greenish-yellow eyes squinted excitedly. "I've heard all about you." I caught my face in their reflection and realized one of my eyebrows was raised, and my mouth was agape.

"Excuse me?"

A big grin spread across her face as if she was about to unleash a huge secret. "I'm Jessica, by the way," she said, sticking out her hand. "Jessica Eris." I reached for it, and she grabbed mine, shaking it firmly.

I nodded curiously. That name sounded familiar.

"Chandra told me you were coming."

Just when I thought her smile couldn't possibly grow any wider, it did. I detached my hand from her firm grip, crossed my arms, and tilted my head again, half amazed and half intrigued.

How did she know Chandra Achelo, one of my good friends at Gaianus? Chandra was a descendant of Achelois, the Moon Goddess who washed away pain. And that was exactly what Chandra did so well for everyone . . . especially the Gods I hurt.

"Okay," I said softly, "please explain how you know me."

She smiled before answering. "Chandra and I knew each other from the Heavens."

"Okay, so you *are* from . . ." I didn't want to say it aloud. "from . . . our Heavens?"

She shook her head exuberantly. "Yeah!" "But isn't this school just for mortals?"

She giggled," Yes, this is a mortal school. But some of *us* go to all-mortal schools—this one in particular. If you are able to keep secrets really well," she said, grinning, "you get used to it—and enjoy it. It's like you know you're better than everyone else."

I nodded. "How long have you lived with them?"

"Thirty years, but," she had to count on her fingers, "it'll be my third year at this school."

"You're a junior then, right?" She nodded. "You?"

"I'm 'transferring in as a sophomore." I quoted the words my mother had told me to use with the admissions counselor. "Some of my credits didn't transfer." I shrugged then chuckled.

She smiled and nodded her head slowly. "How old are you?"

"One hundred and twenty, but just twenty here. How about you?"

"I'll be having my twenty-first birthday on September thirteenth!" She smiled. "For the fifth time."

We both laughed.

I had so many questions to ask her, yet I was stuck on her name. "Jessica Eris . . . Why does that sound so familiar?"

"My ancestor is Eris," she smiled guiltily.

"Eris, that's right," I paused. "Who's Eris again?"

She grinned. "Eris is the Goddess of Discord. She spreader dissension among warriors, politicians—anyone really—just to cause a fight. She was a bitch."

"Sounds awful," I laughed." Is that the gift you have?"

Jessica laughed with me. "Nooo, just the opposite. I am able to create harmony and bring people together through their interests and feelings."

"That's cool," I said enthusiastically. "So when did you last speak to Chandra? How is she doing?"

Jessica gave me an incredulous look. "You haven't spoken to her?" I gave her a long stare back.

"Your mother told Chandra you'd be coming to Regis. So she quickly got a hold of me."

"She told you I'd be coming? What else did she tell you?"

"She said to look for the cocky, confident girl strolling the halls. That'd be her." She grinned crookedly. "But I had a hard time because to me you look more awkward than confident."

I slumped. *Sure am.*

Jessica's face turned contemplative, as if trying to remember Chandra's exact words. "She said to tell you not to worry about Ricky and to get yourself a distraction, maybe a sport. She said you might have fun with it."

I turned my head away from Jessica, gasping at the sound of his name. "She said that?"

"Yeah, hence the reason I got my friend to ask you to play on our soccer team," she said quickly. "So who's Ricky?" The serious expression didn't last long—she was soon grinning again.

"He's my ex-boyfriend. I met him at Gaianus," I replied, my voice fading away. "I broke his heart."

Her lips pressed together, eyebrows showing halfhearted concern. "Yeah, heartbreaker, what makes you say that?"

"Because I felt it breaking," I muttered.

My voice was far away now. My mind raced back to the two of us on that night outside the gates of Gaianus. He was screaming, and I was trying to cry. I felt nothing of me, but everything of him. I felt his heart break and was unable—and unwilling—to catch the pieces, let alone pick them up and put them back together again.

I could not empathize with him, and worst of all, I couldn't feel sadness. I was simply a spectator in my own life. That had always been my problem because that was how I was born . . . without a heart to feel. Emotionally absent. My "gift" was that I could feel everyone's emotions but my own—because I didn't have any.

I had felt his broken heart that night—his tears, his anger, his confusion, and his hurt. I knew he could have loved me,

18

but I'd convinced myself that it must have been a mistake, or was not true love. Everyone falls in love with a challenge. And I had always been the ultimate challenge. Who could fix Petra? Who could make me *feel?* I used to challenge myself as well. I went from God to God, searching for my feelings. I had come the closest with Ricky.

But someone else would be able to treat him better. Someone else was just right for him. I was definitely not the one.

"What do you mean, you felt it?" Jessica's voice brought me back to the present, snapping me out of my reminiscence. I looked up at her bright green eyes, glowing with fascination.

"I can feel what other people are feeling."

She looked up at the ceiling as if deciphering in her head exactly what I meant.

"An empath," I added.

"Got it!" she snapped her fingers.

"But I don't ever feel. But the caveat is I don't feel my own emotions." I gritted my teeth, trying to smile.

"Dang, Pei!" She stopped. "Can I call you Pei?" I laughed. "Sure."

"Well, that's uh . . . that's kind of sad…" She paused. "On a lighter note—" she perked up and looked behind her, then back at me. "You should come to our meeting on Wednesday!"

I shook my head. "I'm good. Thanks, though."

"Are you kidding me? Come on, it'll be fun!"

"We'll see," I said, my resolve already weakening. "But right now, I'd better make it to my next class. Otherwise, I won't be eligible to join any team," I joked, smirking back at her.

Jessica jumped up. "Aw, shoot! You're right!"

We exited the classroom, and I gave her one final nod.

"See you Wednesday?" she asked with a grin.

I smiled back, then shook my head, finally giving in. "Sure. I'll see you Wednesday."

I waved goodbye to her, then turned and started walking down the hallway with a huge smile growing on my face. I had just been played by Jessica Eris 'gifts of Accord.

19

Chapter 4

Orientation

Jessica was waiting for me outside the student center on Wednesday, even though I was early. She saw me and gave me a big, excited wave. "Glad to see you here, lady!"

"Yeah, me too," I shot back sarcastically.

We walked side by side into the conference room. It was set up like a classroom, but instead of desks, there were brown, eight-foot tables lined up with chairs behind them. Jessica and I grabbed two seats close to the front of the room, and she turned around and started waving to someone behind me. I turned to see who it was, and lo and behold, Montana was walking toward us.

This time, she wore a bright maroon Grizzlies shirt and black Grizzlies running shorts, still swinging her Grizzlies lanyard. A walking advertisement, I tell you.

"Petra, you already met Taylor?" Jessica pointed to Montana, who stuck her hand out carelessly and gave me a stiff nod.

So, Montana has a name.

I reached my hand out to hers, just as carelessly. "Not officially," I said. "Hi, I'm Petra Ambrosi." I nodded at her, but she didn't look at me.

"Taylor Letto," she said, and quickly released my hand.

I started to feel something strange in my stomach. I didn't know what it was, but it was the oddest thing I had ever felt. I pulled away and fell back into my chair, watching Taylor—how she talked, her mannerisms. I did not care for the way she used "like" before every sentence. And I had to laugh watching Jessica act like a mortal, though she was reasonably convincing.

I soon grew bored and decided to occupy myself by filling out one of the papers on the table in front of me. I grabbed the one closest to me and began writing. My name, height, and weight were easy, but I paused when I got to "Date of birth" and "Previous school attended."

Stuck, I looked up at Jessica for advice, but she wasn't paying attention, still deep in conversation with Montana. I remembered Jessica saying it was not hard to live with the mortals if you were good at keeping secrets. Did that mean lying, too? I wondered how she'd kept it a secret for so long, especially if she had to fill out paperwork, and decided to wait and see what she wrote rather than make something up.

I looked up from my paper and noticed that many more girls had shown up in the past couple of minutes. You could definitely pick out the newcomers. They were the quiet ones sitting in their chairs, while the veterans remained standing, catching up with people they hadn't seen since the end of the last school year.

A few of them began finding their seats when a very attractive young man walked into the room. I saw Jessica wink at Montana and nod towards the coach before she took her seat next to mine. He must have been in his mid-twenties, about seventy-two inches tall, slightly built, with brown eyes and shaggy, light brown hair. I put my head down and smiled at the emotions I was sensing—there was no doubt every girl in the room felt an attraction to him.

He was followed by two other coaches—a thinner guy with dark, curly hair, very tan, about the same height, and then a short, stocky guy with a round face wearing a hat and holding a clipboard. Obviously the head coach. All three wore blue polo shirts and khaki shorts. They formed a line across the front of the room as they waited for the girls to get to their seats, and the stocky guy ordered us to fill out the sheets in front of us.

Finally, I was able to turn to Jessica for some aid. She looked at me, shook her head, and smiled. Then she leaned over and whispered into my ear, "Put your actual date of birth, but lie about the year."

"Of course." I laughed and then looked back down at the sheet. "What about my previous school?"

"Leave it blank," she whispered back.

The rest of the meeting went by quickly—a couple of exercises to get to know each other, some more paperwork, a folder with our schedule and some inspiring quotes, and a new Regis soccer shirt.

After the orientation, we all piled out of the conference room. I was headed in the direction of the parking lot and my truck until a hand grabbed my arm and I looked up to see Jessica's trademark smile. She pulled me aside.

"Chandra told me that you're good friends with Apria Doves!" I nodded. "I am! How do you know her?"

"Before I came here, I did a little bit of training at Titanus with her." She smiled. "She is quite the Deity."

I had to smile with her, remembering what kind of Goddess Apria was. She was very well known in the Heavens. The Elders said her beauty rivaled that of her ancestor, Aphrodite, and she was undoubtedly the most beautiful creature in existence. Perfection itself could be standing beside her, yet still look heinous in comparison to her beauty. She had very long brown hair that curled down to her chest and lower back, and her skin was a dark olive shade, kissed by Helios the Sun God himself. She had delicate, piercing, sapphire eyes—one look into them would immediately make you melt. Of course, that was what she wanted. That was her power. Everyone loved her. Her beauty was rapture, and her love was ecstasy. And she was deadly.

It was funny to have Apria as a friend. As soon as some new God or Goddess found out who Apria was, they would stare, starstruck. I couldn't blame them. It was a bit uncommon for a deity to have a true inheritance from Titans, Gods, or Goddesses of Cronus or Zeus 'time. Those who did were celebrities. And that was exactly what John, Apria, and my friend Dion were—celebrities.

21

"Hey, Jess," Montana said as she walked up to us. "Want to get dinner at the café?"

"Yeah," Jessica said, and then turned to me, beckoning me to join them.

"No, I'm good. Thank you," I said.

"Oh, come on. You're hungry, right?" Jessica smiled, knowing she had made me agree.

Jessica then turned to Montana and started walking with her down a pathway leading to the center of campus. I gave a sigh and dragged my feet, gradually catching up to them.

We arrived at the café and ordered. I sat down across from Montana while Jessica was at the soft drink dispensers. I caught Montana staring at me a couple of times before quickly looking away. Finally, Jessica returned, ending the awkward stare-and-hide game Montana was playing with me. Shortly after, our food was delivered, and we began eating. All the while, Montana eyed me carefully from across the table.

We left the café, and before Montana could turn the moment into an uncomfortable one, I said, "Hey guys, I'm going to go. Thanks for the invite to dinner. I'll see you tomorrow." I turned around and walked away, hoping to avoid further conversation.

"Well, which way is your dorm?"
I stopped, surprised to hear Montana's voice.

"I'm parked on the west side of campus," I said, pointing in that direction, grateful that I had parked so far from where we were.

"My dorm's over there," she said, and began walking with me.

"I'll see you guys tomorrow," Jessica shouted back to us. She was already halfway to her car.

I looked back at Montana. I was still blown away that she was from the same place I had dreamt of transferring to all summer. Could it be coincidental—or was it fated? Was I making a huge mistake being here? Maybe I still had a chance to leave and go to Titanus?

I was so wrapped up in my thoughts that I almost forgot Montana was walking with me until she spoke. "You remind me of my friend."

"Yeah?" I asked.

"Yes, my friend Ashton Janus." She looked at me, as if confirming her thoughts. "You look almost exactly like her. You act like her, too."

"That's cool," I muttered, and kicked a rock on the ground in front of me. My eyes followed its trajectory, but then the sunset's colors distracted me. They hugged the icy-topped mountains, and the snow reflected the pink.

"You ready for three-a-days tomorrow?" she asked. I noticed she had also stopped walking to watch the sunset with me.

"Three-a-days?" I asked. I must have zoned out during that part of the meeting.

"Yeah, it shouldn't be that bad . . . I mean, if you like running," she said.

I laughed at her serious joke. I hated running.

She swung her head to look at me, eyes wide and curious, maybe a bit surprised. Her gaze crawled up and down, evaluating me. I tried sensing her but got nothing. But when looking into her eyes, I could almost hear her say, *"Who are you?"*

We were just around the corner from her dorm, so I veered in the direction of the parking lot. "Well, I'll see you tomorrow Mont—Taylor." Shit! I almost called her Montana!

She looked up at me with the same curious look she'd had before. I paused, trying to sense anything other than what her expression was giving me. Nothing. I waited a little longer. Still nothing. Was I losing it? If she hadn't broadcast it on her face, I wouldn't have known what she was feeling at all. I gave her a half-smile and began walking away quickly.

"Night," I heard her mumble.

Chapter 5

Three-a-Days

I woke up still tired. It was two in the morning, and it was the longest I'd been able to sleep so far. I didn't know why I couldn't sleep, but I'd been having trouble ever since I arrived at the school. I took a deep breath and sighed. I wished I were at Titanus, but I could say that repeatedly—in many different ways and languages—and it wouldn't help.

Unexpectedly, I began wishing I were at Gaianus. I couldn't believe I had thought it, but it would have been better than being at the mortal school. I was wasting my time here, but I couldn't go back. My mother would be mad.

I unraveled the blanket from around me and sat up in my seat. I relaxed my forehead on the steering wheel for a bit, reminiscing about the summer and the events that had gotten me to where I was. My mother's screams, then my father's, which I had never heard before that night. He was an ancient warrior in his time. I had never seen him cry nor show any kind of emotion, and yet he had screamed with so much pain. The scene kept playing over and over in my head.

My poor mother and father. I had been so naïve to think a scenario like that could never happen to them, to my family. Seeing and feeling my brother in such agony—it had been an unbearably extreme emotion that made him grab Eros 'arrow and drive it through our father's leg.

I looked at the clock and saw it was time to go to practice. I rushed to gather my bag and throw on my practice shirt and shorts. I put my hair up in a messy bun and turned my key in the ignition. The truck roared faithfully to life, and I shook off the haunting screams in my head and began to drive.

∞

I dropped my bag near where Jessica was sitting, tying up her cleats. "Good morning, sunshine!" I said with a smile.

She turned her head to me and smiled back. "Ha! You're a morning person, aren't you?"

"Not at all," I teased.

"Everyone!" The stocky coach was walking up to the team, followed by the other two. "Ladies, don't put on your cleats just yet!"

The veterans moaned. The other half of the team, the newbies, looked around curiously. I sensed the veterans were peeved as they began putting their cleats away and taking out their running shoes. I searched through my threadbare bag and found my running shoes flattened at the bottom. Pulling them out, I slipped my right shoe on first, followed by my left, but my toes jammed up against something at the tip.

I pulled my foot out quickly and shook my shoe until something fell out onto the grass. I smiled. It was my old chicken wire bracelet, and hanging from it was the single good luck charm Ricky had given me on our first date—a bronze myrtle piece with the number *13* etched on the back.

I had a flashback of Ricky grabbing his crotch while saying, "There must have been two of you." A disgusting gesture with good intentions. Ricky had been referencing the famous story of Aphrodite's birth: Ouranos ' own son, Cronus, castrated him, and both of Ouranos 'testicles fell into the sea, causing it to foam—and out of the foam appeared Aphrodite.

Ricky used to say that since both of Ouranos 'testicles fell, then not one, but two Goddesses were created. He joked that I was the *thirteenth* Goddess (an addition to the first twelve Gods and Goddesses of Olympus)— and Aphrodite's sister. The myrtle was Aphrodite's sign. It was quite dramatic and highly unlikely, but possibly the sweetest thing anyone had ever said to me.

I threw the bracelet back in my bag, squelching the memory, put on my shoes, and quickly ran off to join the team.

∞

Day one of three-a-days, and the first practice was already hell.

Fortunately, it was coming to an end. Our captains called us into a circle to stretch, and I planted myself between a girl whose name I had already forgotten and Montana. I caught her staring at me again, and then laughed when she tried to pretend she wasn't. I nodded, and she smiled back.

After practice, I veered off to the side, where I had purposely left my bag away from everyone else's. I had removed my cleats and was ready to go when I saw Jessica and Montana coming toward me.

"Not bad, eh?" Jessica asked, slapping my back and giving me a sure smile.

"Not bad so far," I said. "Only two more sessions today."

"What are you up to now before the second session?"

I stared at Jessica, thinking she had asked the question, but then I looked at Montana and realized it was she who had spoken.

"Oh, nothing, I guess. I suppose I'll go get some food," I said, trying not to sound as though I was caught off-guard, even though I was.

"Well, you can hang out at my dorm until the next practice," she said carefully, looking at the grass. "I can make us something to eat."

"Yeah, sure . . ." I eyed her, and then looked at Jessica. "What are you about to do, Jess?"

"I'm going back home to finish sleeping," she said, laughing.

That sounded nice to me as well, but then again, no matter how much I tried, I was sure I could not fall asleep.

"Okay. Did you walk here?" I asked, staring at Montana. She still averted her eyes, and I began playing a game with myself, silently daring her to look.

"Um . . . yeah," she said. "Would it be okay . . .

" I waited for her to ask what she wanted to ask, humored by her struggle. ". . . if I rode with you . . . back to the dorm?" she finally spat out.

I gawked at her for a minute, valiantly trying to refrain from laughing. "Yeah, no problem," I assured her, holding my hand up to my mouth to hide my smile.

We started walking to the parking lot, Montana staying an uneasy step behind me. Finally, we reached my truck, and I quickly climbed into the driver's seat. She struggled to get in.
She's so awkward.

"Thanks for giving me a ride," she said once settled in the seat. I looked over and saw her staring out the windshield, as if she was thanking *it* and not me.

"Yeah, of course," I said. "Thank you for inviting me to hang out."

"Well, where were you going to go?" She snickered.

"I don't know," I said. "I was just going to drive around."

"Oh," she said quietly.

There was a second or two of awkward silence. I could see her studying me from the corner of my eye.

"You sure do stare at me a lot," I finally blurted out.
Her lips shifted apart and her body went rigid. Finally, she answered in a stutter, "Y-you seem familiar to me."

"Right," I said, "like your friend, you said."

She sat back in her seat and pondered. I thought she would reply, but she remained quiet for the rest of the drive. When we reached the parking lot at her dorm, I cut the engine and hopped out of the truck. Montana slid out of her seat, stretching her feet out until her toes hit the pavement.

We took a pathway toward the building, which was actually a collection of townhouses called the Residence Village. The pathway split between two rows of two-story, red brick townhouses. Trees were planted along the paths leading up to each doorway. We turned onto the second walkway on the left, and I followed her up the stairs to the second floor, where we stopped at her door.

She scrambled around in her Montana Grizzlies bag for the keys. When she found them, she tugged, and they came flinging out. She awkwardly put her key in the lock, fumbling to get it in the keyhole. Finally, it unlocked, and she swung the door open.

Her place was spacious and well-furnished for a college student's residence. There were two large, circular chairs in the living room instead of sofas and a twenty-inch flat screen television in front of them.

"So what would you like for lunch? Or brunch?" Montana asked nervously.

"I don't care. What were you planning on having?" I walked over to the chairs and plopped down in one of them.

"I have some rice, and...

26

" She went to the refrigerator and opened the freezer. She looked for a while and finally pulled out a bag. "Peas?"

"Peas are good," I said. "Want anything to drink?" "Water is fine. Thank you."

As she prepared our meal, I noticed something unusual. Everything was quiet—not sound, but emotion. That was a first. Ever. I was unsure if it was even real. My eyes closed, and I focused harder on her emotions. Then I smiled. There were none. It was indescribably peaceful.

My eyes opened, and I saw her staring at me. She handed me a plate and then sat down in the chair next to me. I thanked her and began to eat. She did as well, very deliberately lifting the spoon to her mouth, and then slowly dropping it back to her plate, all the while eying me intensely. Every so often, I would look up, nod my head, smile, chew, and sip my water. We said nothing. The peace I thought I liked was becoming a bit unusual.

Suddenly, the front door flew open and two girls stumbled in, talking and laughing loudly. They were tall and slender, athletically built, and beautiful.

"Tayyyyyy!" They both screamed excitedly.

"Hey guys." She laughed shyly.

"You're alive! Thank God," one of them joked, giving Montana a big hug. "How was the first practice so far?" the other added.
"Good. Not bad at all."

They finally noticed me, and instantly pivoted and stared.

"Hi," I said, waving to them.

"That's Petra, guys. She's on the soccer team with me," Montana told them. "These are my roommates, Tawny and Sade."

"Hey!" they said simultaneously, and then continued talking and laughing as they headed down the hallway to their bedrooms.

Montana picked up our plates and headed toward the kitchen. She looked confused, trying to find where to put our dishes. She ultimately decided to leave them on the counter and then returned to her chair. We stared at each other for a bit without saying a word. During that silence, I still didn't sense anything from her.

"So where are you staying?" she asked. It was what I was afraid of, but I knew I would have to deal with it sooner or later. Unlike Jessica, I did not like secrets or lying. I paused for a bit before answering.
"In my truck," I said. I took the hair tie off my wrist and started fidgeting with it.

"You're staying in your truck? As in . . . sleeping in it?"

"Yeah." I was still fidgeting.

"Why?"

"Why not?" I asked.

"Why don't you stay here?

" She made it sound as if I should have thought of that.

"Because I have my truck," I told her, tone stern. I stopped fidgeting with my hair tie and looked up at her. She was looking back at me strangely.

"Okay . . ." she said softly. "Well, you're always welcome."

Chapter 6

Scar Face

I never did take Montana up on her offer. Occasionally, I would ask to take a shower at her place, but other than that, I had my truck, and that was all I needed. Our soccer season was halfway over, with only five games left. Then we had playoffs—if we made it that far.

Our team wasn't doing badly, but we weren't doing extremely well, either. Jessica and Montana were amazing in the midfield—as were Jaden and Diane, who played defense. They were extremely weird . . . friendly and nice, but weird. I wasn't doing too well, but thankfully the other forward, Madison, helped me look half-decent. She always put the ball exactly where my feet were. It amazed me each time.

One weekend we didn't have a game, so we decided to head out of town. On my way to pick up Montana, I noticed that the sky was clear, which was quite unusual in October. I gazed at the oak trees hugging the sides of the road, getting lost in their autumn colors. I had just flicked my left blinker on when I saw flashing red and blue neon lights in the rearview mirror. I looked down at my speedometer. 70 mph. Then I saw the speed limit sign. 45 mph. I was only a mile from school, too.

I pulled over near a gas station and shut down my angry engine. I had no idea what would happen next. Would he suspect I was different? I watched the cop get off his motorcycle with a pad of paper and pen. How was I supposed to give him my information? I still hadn't completed all the mortal papers for a driver's license and car registration, so I was most certainly doomed.

He reached my car and tapped on my window. I rolled it down slowly. Without any small talk, he asked for my driver's license, insurance, and registration. I took out a piece of paper and handed it to him.

He looked up from his pad, waiting. "Driver's license and insurance?" he sneered.

I looked at him. He had a thick scar on the bottom of his chin that mesmerized me—it must have been a deep cut. I stared at the scar while contemplating whether to run or lie, but I could do neither.

"I-I don't have them," I whispered, sounding guilty.

"Why don't you have them?" He was shouting now. His scar curved upward with his sneering lip.

"I do." The words popped out before I could stop them.

"You do?" His eyebrow rose, and he stepped back.

"Y-y-e-e . . ." I could not even form the word.

"You mean your license is suspended? Are you driving on a suspended license?"

"Yes." The halting reply I had been trying to form finally emerged, answering the wrong question.

"Oh really?" he said. I sensed his anger, invisibly swirling out through his nose and ears. "Ma'am, please step out of the vehicle."

I felt like a dog with its tail between its legs as I hopped out of my truck and stared at the ground.

"Ma'am, I'm giving you a ticket for speeding, for driving on a suspended license, and for no proof of insurance." He tore the ticket off his pad and handed it to me. "And now we're going to have to tow your truck."

I looked into his eyes and sensed it all, every emotion. Suddenly, something familiar tingled my senses. It came from behind him. I stared past him, trying to identify it, and then smiled once I understood. It was Jessica and another girl on our soccer team. Britta's shocked freckled face showed her pity for me, but Jessica was laughing. Of course.

I smiled at her, shaking my head. Seeing her laugh brought out the humor in the situation—decades of being an invincible Goddess, only to be shut down by Scar Face, a mortal police officer. It was my first lesson in being a human, and it sucked.

"Do you have anyone who can pick you up?" His condescending tone suddenly changed from boorish to polite, like he really cared. How odd—such a sudden change within seconds.

"Yes," I told him, "they're over there." I nodded to Jessica, and she nodded back.

I smiled at the officer politely, said goodbye to my truck, and walked to Jessica and Britta, pondering how the officer's emotion could have changed so abruptly. But then I realized it had been Jessica's gift of Accord, changing his emotion to match hers.

Britta rushed up and hugged me in consolation. I looked over her head and laughed with Jessica, who was still laughing at me.

The rush of Britta's worry rang in my ears as she stepped back to look at me. "Why are they taking your truck?"

I grinned, and Jessica grinned with me. "I don't have a license."

"You what?" she asked, shocked.

"Yeah," I told her. "I guess this means we should call the girls—I won't be coming with you guys."

Jessica laughed. "Not a chance! You need to get your truck back."

"Where are they taking it?" Britta asked.

Jessica grabbed my shirt and pushed me toward her car. "They're taking it to the tow yard. Come on, I'll take you there."

∞

I left the tow yard without my truck, thinking about the mess I was in. My truck was my home, my bed, my closet . . .my freedom.

30

Jessica quickly sidled up next to me. "Don't worry about it. You'll get it back in a year. Question is, where are you going to live until then?"

"You can live with me," Britta jumped in without thinking twice; it was amazing to watch Jessica use her gifts. "I just leased out a small house with Jaden and Diane."

Jessica and I both smirked. Jaden Krowe and Diane Wading were the Earthly equivalent of Poseidon's Nymphets: young teenage women who lived in water and were very, very desirable—and aware of their popularity among mortal men.

I leaned over to whisper into Jessica's ear, "Nymphets, for sure." We both laughed.

"We move in October eighth," Britta continued. "You can stay with me until then."

There was a reason I preferred to be alone. My gift was great, and I was blessed that it had been bestowed on me, but it did have its negatives. Being around people—mortal or immortal—was very noisy and sometimes made me feel as if I was riding a never-ending emotional rollercoaster—all day, *every* day.

It was distressing to feel people's reactions to everything that affected them. The most prevalent mortal emotions were worry and fear—mainly fear. They feared everything. It was overwhelming at times—and annoying—and that was just from being around them during the school day. I couldn't imagine what it would be like actually share a living space with them. At the end of the day, when I was finally alone, I was at peace. I sensed no worries, no fear, nothing.

"No, I'll figure it out. Thank you, though."

Jessica shot me a look. "Petra, where else are you going to stay?"

I stared back at her and felt the pull of her gifts trying to make me give in.

"Okay," I agreed, exasperated. I had nowhere else to stay anyway.

31

Chapter 7

The Question Game

I stared at the projector blankly, my hand holding my head up and my fingers tangled in my uncombed hair as I scratched my scalp. The professor shuffled through another slide, rambling on. I glanced back down at my desk and realized I had not written a single note, just scribbled thoughts, and verses from what I assumed was a poem. But the verses were scattered and didn't make any sense.

I turned to a blank sheet of paper and finally started copying down notes from the current slide—number 23 out of 30. I must have zoned out for quite a while. I couldn't believe I had missed so much.

At two minutes past the end of our allotted class time, I closed my binder, slid it into my backpack, and zipped it up.

"Miss Ambrosi, are you going somewhere?"

I stared back at the professor dully, surprised he even knew my name. "No, Dr. Griffin, not anymore," I said, unzipping my backpack and smiling politely. "I don't mind being late to my next class."

I felt bursts of mute laugher scattered throughout the classroom, but everyone remained quiet, only the smirks on their faces giving them away.

He faltered, clearly not knowing what to say. Tapping his pen on his palm a couple of times, he finally said, "Okay. You guys are free to go. We'll pick this up tomorrow."

Tomorrow was our last game of the season. It would decide whether or not we made it to playoffs.

"Dr. Griffin," I said hesitantly, "I won't be here tomorrow. It's our last game of the season."

"Who's we?" he snapped.

I sank down in my seat. "The soccer team?"

He shook his head. "Well then, you'll just have to get the notes from somebody in class."

Great. I don't know anyone in class.

I slung my backpack hastily over my shoulder, and it hit my back harder than I'd expected. I sighed. I had a collection of heavy books, papers to write, tests to study for—all on topics I had absolutely no interest in.

Mortal college was a lot harder than I had imagined.

I walked out the doorway into the cool Colorado breeze. We were having unexpectedly great weather. The sky was a bright blue with not a single cloud in sight, and the leaves on the oak trees around campus had completely changed to brilliant reds, oranges, and yellows.

Around campus, students had begun putting up flyers for Halloween costume parties and contests. People were hanging decorations on windows and inside classrooms. Orange and black were everywhere. I smiled to myself. Halloween was one of Dion's favorite holidays to go Heaven hopping.

Heaven hopping was a tradition for the three of us—Apria, Dion, and me. Whenever we had a break from training—or spontaneously decided to take a trip—we would choose which Heaven we wanted to visit from one of Earth's many portals. Every Halloween, one specific portal opened—the Draco portal, a Heaven that was like home to Dion.

His ancestor, Dionysus, was half Draco and half Olympian God. He was one of the Twelve Olympians, the God of Wine and Ecstasy, the creator of crazy parties. There were many very strange and elaborate stories about how he was born.

The story I heard was that Zeus had an affair with a mortal woman named Semele. In ancient times, it was said that mortals could not bear to look upon the face of Zeus, for his power was too great for mortal eyes to behold. Therefore, the affair between Semele and Zeus was conducted during the darkest hours of the night. One night, however, once she became impregnated with Dionysus, Semele came to Zeus, asking to see his face, to see the father of her child—an honest and fair request, even though gazing upon him would cause her incineration. Nevertheless, at her insistence, Zeus could not deny her, so he revealed himself—as little as possible in order not to cause harm. But his greatness and light were still too overwhelming, and she was instantly consumed in flame, disintegrating to dust. In order to preserve the fetus, Zeus sewed Dionysus into his thigh, and a few months later, Dionysus was born— again.

Once Dion grew older and began his training at Titanus, he delved deeper into his ancestral line and discovered more about himself than most Deities I knew. With help from Bacchants and some Maenads, he discovered that Semele was from the Draco portal, and from that information, another story was revealed. It was not Zeus 'great power that had incinerated Semele, but the light. Humans would not perish when looking upon Zeus, but Vrykolakas—or Drakanons—would. Vampires.

Dionysus had been sewn into Zeus 'thigh so that he could feed from his blood for strength. The Vrykolakas were known in other human cultures by different names. In Native American cultures, they were called witches or shape shifters. Semele and other Vrykolakas were able to turn themselves into wolves, leopards, lizards—pretty much anything they wanted. Some of the Olympian Gods shared this power, but none exploited it as much as the Vrykolakas, torturing and scaring humans with their many disguises. Vrykolakas are just one of the many strange creatures that come from the Draco portal. And when opened up, a whole new world of fear is released for the mortals. For some reason, Dion loved it.

I could still remember our first Halloween night. It was in the 1900s, and we had decided to go to New York City for the first time. It was also our first time traveling down to Earth for one of their holidays. We were very young and naïve—novice Deities. I could still remember the mortals '

33

expressions when they looked at us. Everyone stared. We were asked so many questions: Were we royalty? Freaks? From a different continent? They were not far off. We were just from a different world.

However, most people stared at us because of Apria. Life came to a halt whenever she entered a room, or simply strolled outside. Time seemed to stand still while everyone admired her.

I was never jealous of the stares meant just for her the way that other Goddesses were. I believed that beauty was never a great thing—it was a lonely thing. I felt sorry for her. It was less awful—in my opinion—to be a great Goddess and have everyone kneel at your feet, than to be a beautiful Goddess and have everyone just stare and not say a thing. That would be annoying and, in some cases, scary.

When I first encountered Apria as a child, I thought she was the cockiest, most annoying creature I had ever met. However, her cockiness turned out to be educational. She was the one who taught me about beauty, and she was the first to tell me I was beautiful. Not in the way a parent would tell a daughter, but in a way so sincere and genuine, it made me believe it to be true. She would always praise my wavy blonde hair and blue eyes. I never thought there was anything special about my beauty compared to hers, yet she made me feel like there was. She made me see it. I smiled at the thought. I supposed I missed her and Dion . . . just a little.

My next class was Greek. I was crossing the street toward the building where my class met when I saw Montana on the other side. I began to turn around, but then I heard her call my name.
"Hey, Brosi!"
It was the nickname the soccer team had given me. The girls thought they were clever in making it up, but the Deities at Gaianus had been calling me that for decades. It sounded somehow different coming from Montana, though.

" How's your day so far?" she asked. As sunny as it was outside, she still wore a hoodie and jeans.

"It's . . . good," I answered. "How about yours?"

She hesitated a second, and then smiled. "If you think being tortured by a professor is fun…" she shrugged, "then it's going great."

I laughed. "You too, huh? I'm pretty sure Dr. Griffin is drawing an 'F ' on my report card as we speak."

She chuckled, but then stopped, as if I had said something sad. "Yeah," she said, pityingly.

"Are you alright?" I asked, trying to catch her eyes.

"Of course!" Her head snapped up. "I'm good. Why wouldn't I be?" She smiled again.

Maybe my expression was rude because she shot me a look like I said something inappropriate. Trying to correct whatever I had done wrong, I said, "Hey, let's have a study session tonight and watch the Montana football game!" I tried my best to sound enthusiastic to lighten up the strange conversation, and her expression brightened instantly.

"That'd be fun, but we actually have to study. I can never study when you come over," she teased.

I laughed. "Okay, I'll see you tonight."

I turned to leave, but she grabbed my arm. My breath paused suddenly, as if her hand had stolen the air I was about to inhale.

"Wait," she said, quietly. "What are you doing for dinner?"

I hadn't noticed it before, but in that moment, I realized it was the very first time she had touched me since we shook hands on our first meeting. For the past couple of months, I had become pretty close with her—hanging out after practices, dinners after games, and study sessions in her dorm room and the library. She was my favorite person to hang out with for one specific reason—I could not sense her emotions, and that gave me peace. And throughout all of those times we hung out, she had never laid a finger on me, but as she held onto my arm, I felt something from her that rendered me speechless. All I could reply with was an unsteady shake of my head.

"Want to come over early?" she asked uneasily. "We can walk to Sunflower Market and get some things to make dinner?"

I think I forgot how to use my lips—I could not get them to move. My mind was still stuck on trying to understand what it was I had sensed from her light touch.

"Ye-Yeah," I finally spat out.

"Okay," she said with a smile.

She released my arm—and instantly the feeling was gone.

∞

We met outside her townhouse. The sun had been swallowed up by the gray sky, and a cool breeze flowed across my face and neck.
Montana was standing outside with her back to me, warming herself with her folded arms while looking at the storm clouds.

"Hey," I said as I walked up to her.

She turned around, smiling pensively. "Hey."

She uncrossed her arms and started playing with her hood, putting it to the side of her neck and wrapping her fingers in it as if it was her hair. For some strange reason, where she placed her hood caught my attention, and immediately I fell into a sort of trance as we began to walk off campus.

"So have you been seeing anyone?" I heard her ask, bringing my focus back.

I shook my head. "No." There was a long pause before I asked, "How are you and Ryan doing? Are you guys officially—?"

"No," she said curtly, cutting me off.

It must have been a sore subject, but that only intrigued me more. "May I ask why?"

She looked at me for a second. "It's a long story." She paused. "Basically, it's just never going to happen."

"Oh," I said. "Then why do you guys even hang out?"

She shot me an exasperated look. "Because he's a cool guy to hang out with. But we don't hook up!" she blurted, as if knowing I was going to ask that next.

I laughed. "Why do you say it's a long story? That seems pretty short to me."

She stared at the pavement, absorbed in her own thoughts. "Just is," she said softly.

It must have been something emotional, although I couldn't tell. Not only did she not emit emotion, but her thoughts were blocked as well. I decided to stop prying.

I wanted us to touch again, to see if I could sense anything from her— or maybe experience again the mysterious feeling I had sensed from her earlier. I swung my arm forward in an attempt to connect with hers. We touched, but I felt nothing. I gestured toward absolutely nothing to the left of us in an attempt to touch her shoulder. Again, I felt nothing. I gave up, and instead stared at the side of her face to see if I could read it. She turned and caught my stare.

"What are you looking at?"

I shook my head and answered softly, "Thought I saw something."

∞

We left the market with more than we had gone in for. I was carrying a bag with two loaves of bread that smelled like cinnamon rolls. Montana and I thought they looked too good not to eat, so we'd decided on that for dessert.

The walk back to school was not as silent as the walk to the market had been. Montana made up something she called the question game. We took turns firing random questions back and forth.

"If you could choose love or fame, which would you choose?" she asked.

"I would choose love," I said.

She gave me an exasperated look. "What? No way!"

"What would you pick?" I asked, laughing.

"No, you can't ask the same question back, remember?" "Okay." I grinned, trying to think of another question. "Why did you pick love?" she asked, sounding intrigued.

"It's my turn to ask a question," I teased. She rolled her eyes, and I laughed. "I've never been in love. I'm interested in what it feels like, I guess."

She slowly lifted her head and tilted it, not saying anything. It looked like she wanted to, though.

We had reached the steps to her townhouse, and she started fumbling for her keys. After a while, she finally fished the Grizzlies lanyard out of a Grizzlies gym sack, unlocked the door, and pushed it open.

"Hey, Tay! Hey, Brosi!" I heard from inside.

We walked farther into the living room and the intoxicating scent of vanilla hit our noses. We followed the shouts and found Tawny and Sade standing in the kitchen, frosting all over their faces.

"Hey guys! What are you making?" I approached the kitchen counter and eyed the bowl of white frosting.

Tawny's face brightened. "We're making vanilla cake with vanilla frosting and sprinkles!" She removed another cake from the refrigerator, placed it on the counter, and started frosting the golden top.

"You made two?" Montana asked, her eyes widening.

"Yes! Tawny made one for Brian, and I made one for Jason," Sade said, with a big smile. "We're about to head over to their place and surprise them."

I walked over to one of the sofas, which had replaced the two circular chairs, and put the loaves of cinnamon bread on the small wooden table. "Our dessert looks better," I said, helping myself to a piece.

Montana smiled, walked to the other sofa, and plopped herself down.

We sat eating in silence long enough for me to catch wind of Sade and Tawny's curious emotions. I pressed my lips together in an attempt to stop my smile. Montana reached over and turned on the football game, then reached for another slice of cinnamon bread.

"Alright, guys, we're going downstairs," Sade announced a short while later, holding one of the cakes in her hand.

Montana hopped up from the couch. "See you guys tomorrow night then?"

They both just laughed as they headed out the door.

Montana went to the kitchen to start prepping our meal, and I got my books out.

"So, back to the question game," she said as she set a pot of water on the stove to boil.turn."

I laughed. She sure did love playing games. "Okay. I think it's your

"So you said you've never been in love . . .?"

I stopped flipping through my book and looked over at her. "Yeah?" "Why?" she asked. Her head tilted again. "Have you just not tried—or what?"

I smiled. "No, I've just never felt it."

She narrowed her eyes, clearly wanting more of an explanation.

"I mean . . ." I had no way of explaining that I couldn't feel love, only sense it in others, yet I wanted to try. "I believe there are three different kinds of love . . . and I think most often people get mistaken and confused about which one they are feeling . . ."

"Three?" she asked.

"I don't know," I mumbled, shaking my head. "It's just a theory."

"I want to hear it."

I looked at her, and our eyes met. I still couldn't sense a single thing from her. She was a locked vault that I could not open.

"Well," I began, taking a deep breath. "I believe there is the unconditional love deep within your soul that you have for your family. No matter how much you think you hate them or how angry you get with them, you are always going to love them—even if you're in denial about that."

Montana nodded as if she agreed with that.

"Then there is the respect and caring kind of love you have for your friends— love borne of the mind," I explained. "I believe it then becomes like an equation—joining the two. Like with your best friend, then you love someone unconditionally with both your mind and your soul."
I paused, but she beckoned me to continue.

"Finally, there's intimate love—an attraction, an infatuation. You show this love physically with your body. This is where people get confused. Again, I think it's like an equation. Say you love a friend, but also are attracted to them and try to make it an intimate relationship, combining mind and body. I think that will only equal lust, and relationships like that never

last because the soul has to be added, too—the unconditional love part." I took a deep breath. "Not until all three—mind, body, and soul—are combined will it equal the truest essence of love. If you find yourself not coerced, and truly *in* love, it will never go away."

Montana looked confused but interested, and she waved for me to go on.

"No matter how much you want it to, or how much you try to forget, or try to deny it, the love runs too deeply into your soul for it to die. Because everyone's soul lives forever, you can never get rid of it." I sighed. "So, I'm waiting for a love like that."

She was quiet, her mouth slightly agape.

"It's only a theory," I said, "but a theory I live by, which is challenging for some of the G. . ." I caught myself, " . . . *guys* I have dated who thought they were *in* love with me. I always thought they were oblivious to their own true feelings. When it is true love, I believe both people will feel the *same* love with one another. Although, I've never been intimate enough with anyone to really know."

"Wait," she said. "Are you saying you're a virgin?"

I was ready for that reaction. I had gotten it from many Deities before. Apria and Dion were my biggest bullies. I could hear Apria's words of advice: "*Petra, seriously! Go out and do it with the first God you want. It really isn't a big deal.*" But it was. I believed you were not just giving away your body, you were giving a piece of your soul—each time . . . every time. I wanted to give my soul only to the one I loved.

I laughed to myself. Over a century old, and I was finally face to face with the first mortal to judge me. I leaned back on the couch, ready for her teasing. "Yes."

She did not do what I expected. Instead she came over and sat down next to me, smiling softly. "So am I."

" Are you waiting, too?" I asked, surprised.

"No." She shook her head. "Well, I suppose. I just haven't found the right guy yet."

We heard the pot boiling over, sloshing steaming water onto the stovetop, and Montana stood quickly and went back to the kitchen.

I lay down on the couch and watched her prepare dinner. She threw in the spaghetti noodles and then prepared the sauce in another pot, tasting it every so often to see if it was just right. Just then, she reminded me of my mother—my beautiful, pure mother whom I had been horribly neglecting for nearly three months. I had to wonder if she was doing okay, and if Father, John, and Eva were well, too.

I felt my eyes begin to get heavy as I played memories of my family in my head. And before they finally closed, a thought surfaced. *I miss them.*

Chapter 8

Game Day

Startled from sleep by the slam of a door, I popped up from where I had lain on the couch. For a second, I forgot where I was until I remembered I was in Montana's townhouse.

There was a blanket tucked underneath me, and a pillow where my head had rested. I was still half asleep, but it was the best sleep I'd had since coming to Colorado.

Something caught my eye on the table in front of me. A folded piece of paper with my name written on it. I reached for the paper, opened it, and began reading.

Petra,

   Sorry for making you late to class—I didn't want to wake you up. You just looked so angelic sleeping there. Text me when you're up so I know you're alive. Have a good day today! See you at the game.

- Taylor

I got up from the couch and looked down at my wrinkled clothes. Rubbing my eyes, I headed to the bathroom, bracing myself before looking in the mirror. My ponytail was pushed to the side, drooping loosely over my ear. I leaned over the sink to get a closer look at my face. It was not glowing now, but pale as ever. I stepped away from the mirror to look at my clothes. My sweatshirt was covered in powdered sugar and cinnamon from the bread we had eaten last night, and my jeans were wrinkled and dirty.

I laughed. If Apria and Dion ever caught me wearing this in public, I would never hear the end of it. The highly chic duo lived their lives in a never-ending fashion show—they sported flashy colors and high-fashion designs when on Earth and were entirely too stylish to be hanging out with the likes of me. I had no idea why they wanted to be seen with me. I was totally on the other end of the fashion spectrum. I kept it simple—tank top or T-shirt and jeans. I had never cared too much about the impression I made, though, because—obviously—I *couldn't*.

∞

My classes whizzed by. It felt as if I was standing still and everything else was going in fast-forward around me. I had only one interest, and that was our soccer game. I couldn't recall how I got to my classrooms, what was taught, or even how I ended up in the locker room.

As I entered, though, I felt all my teammates.

40

I stepped into their nervous fog and felt the tension seeping out of each and every pore. At practice, we'd been reminded that the game would determine whether we would go to playoffs. A clean and simple win was all we needed.

Scanning the locker room, I looked for the most isolated seat and found an empty bench down an aisle of lockers. I tossed my bag onto it and began to undress.

"You're alive," Montana said from behind me.

I spun around and saw her smiling brilliantly.

"Yeah," I said softly. She has the most beautiful smile. "You didn't text me."

I tilted my head when realizing that out of the whole time hanging with Montana, we never exchanged number.

"I don't even have your num—"

The coaching staff entered and yelled for us, and so Montana left me, scurrying to find a spot in the huddle. After a few motivational words from the coaches, we piled out of the locker room and onto the field.

Madison stood next to me as we both prepared ourselves for the beginning kickoff. She gave me a cocky smile and nod. With that single nod, I felt her confidence and eagerness to play. I grinned back at her as the whistle blew.

The kickoff began. I kicked the ball to Madison, who passed it to Jessica at midfield. I sprinted up the left sideline as Jessica quickly passed to Montana on her left. Without a dribble, Montana wound up her leg, threw it back, and then snapped it forward. She contacted the ball hard, and it flew up the line to me, a perfect pass directly to my feet.

I dribbled up the sideline, feeling Madison's excitement. I looked up and saw her wide open in the center of the goalkeeper's box. As a defender ran toward me, I caught a whiff of her fear, so I made a single juke to the left, crossed to my right, and kicked the ball as hard as I could to the center, hoping the ball would land somewhere near Madison. I watched it fly to where she stood, the tallest in the middle of three defenders. The ball floated to her, seemingly in slow motion. At the perfect time, Madison jumped to greet it. Her feet lifted nearly to the hips of her surrounding opponents. They tried to jump to the ball as well, but Madison got there first, snapping her head and directing the ball where she wanted it.

It seemed like minutes, but it actually took only a few seconds for Madison to blast the ball past the keeper's fingertips and into the upper corner of the goal. Without celebration, Madison ran down the center of the field, smiled at me, and asked, "Again?"

That was a wakeup call for our opponents. I felt their anger instantly—and it remained a constant. Back and forth, the game continued with intensity, but the score remained 1-0. It soon turned into a bloody battle. Girls from both teams slammed their bodies against one another, desperate for the ball, hands scratching and tearing at jerseys and hair.

41

Finally, the defender who had been guarding me the entire first half unleashed the aggravation I had felt building up inside her. I was running, trying to get open for my team's throw-in, when she shoved me from behind. I had been expecting it, and now that it had happened, I turned and smiled at her. That made her even angrier. She swung at my face, but I bobbed my head to the side, and her fist went flying past my cheek. She made a second attempt, nearly hitting the referee as he grabbed her. She was given a red card, and my coach yelled for me to get off the field.

As I ran off, I sensed his anger. He pointed to the bench without looking at me. Things were getting too heated and too close for me to be pissing off the other team, I supposed. I looked up to see if he had anything more to say, but he did not.
He called to Montana, "Taylor! Taylor! Take Petra's spot! Jaden! Move up to Taylor's spot!"

I watched from the sideline as the new formation developed. Taylor was just as fast as I was and would surely beat the defender who had replaced the angry one.

Suddenly, a burning lance struck the right side of my body, and I turned to see the angry defender glaring furiously at me from the opposing bench. I stared back at her, feeling her anger intensify. There was no way for me to arrest her fire. But then suddenly, something did.

A scream carried across the field. Quickly, she detached her stare and turned toward the sound.   I looked as well and discovered my whole bench and the entire coaching staff standing on the sideline. I walked toward the wall of players, sensing the horror, worry, and fear. As I pushed through, I had no doubt I was going to witness something traumatic. And I did.

Four trainers rushed to assist one of our Regis players lying on the field. Some of my team left the sideline and raced toward the injured player. I could not make out who it was, so I slowly strode onto the field as well. As I reached the group huddled around the downed player, I saw that some of my teammates had started to tear up. My eyes traveled around the circle of girls, sensing each one's emotion. Finally, I bent down, trying to get a closer look. I darted my eyes around the hovering trainers and met Montana's tortured eyes. I think time paused for a moment as I watched her writhing in pain. And yet, even as her suffering eyes pierced mine, I still could not feel her emotion. I shifted my eyes from her face down to her body, trying to understand what she clutched. It was her chest—she was grabbing her chest.

I didn't understand. My eyes swept the circle, searching for Jessica, but I couldn't find her. I looked back down at Montana, back at her hand gripping her chest, and found her other hand holding someone else's. I followed the

hand upward to Jessica. She was kneeling next to the head trainer, gripping Montana's hand tightly, and looking into Montana's eyes. I sensed her—calm and in control.

42

I twisted my neck to get a better look at Montana's face and saw her become more composed. Her eyes were less tortured, but her teeth were still clenched tightly. Slowly, Jessica's powers were easing Montana's pain and worry, and they began noticeably changing the emotions of the rest of the team as well.

Soon an ambulance arrived on the field, and men in blue uniforms rushed out to assist Montana, who was now lying calmly on the ground. It took only a couple of minutes for them to get her strapped on a stretcher and placed in the ambulance, which drove away with sirens wailing.

No one had time to discuss what had just happened—the whistle blew to get the game started again, and there was no mention of it on the bench.

Our coaches and players focused on the game in front of them.

I spent the rest of the game on the bench with Madison and Jessica. It seemed that only the three of us cared about what had happened to Montana— we sat, dazed and confused. I had all but forgotten about the game until I heard the final whistle. I looked at the scoreboard: 2-1. We only had the one goal we'd scored in the very beginning. I couldn't recall how the other team had scored two, but they had beaten us and won our desired spot in the playoffs.

Jessica sat up quickly after the whistle blew, looking at me with concern in her eyes. "Let's go see Taylor at the hospital."

We were gone before the other players had even left the field.

Chapter 9

The Hospital Visit

I had never been to a hospital. For a century, I had done a great job avoiding them, and now I knew why. It was exactly what I had expected.

Jessica looked back at me before walking through the doors. "Prepare yourself."

I inhaled deeply and entered. Within seconds, I was devoured by sorrow. My ears pulsated with the pain. I looked at every face in the waiting room and heard each internal hardship. Crying, screaming, begging—the emotions were so heavy and so strong that they caused a constant ringing in my ears.

It got worse. As we made our way down the hall, it was as if we were walking past explosives—a disease causing extreme suffering, an agonizing illness, a tormenting disorder, the grief of loss. The hallways felt miles long. I squeezed my eyes shut. My hands covered my ears as I tried to shut it all out.

I smiled when I felt nothing and slowly opened my eyes. I knew we had to be getting close to Montana's room. Jessica gently grabbed my shoulder, and my weakened gaze unclouded once I saw Montana's face. She sat up in bed as soon as she saw us. Her small smile grew gradually larger and her eyes widened as she stared at us in disbelief.

"I can't believe you guys came," she said.

Jessica laughed, and I chuckled easily, gratefully. The atmosphere was finally bearable, and I could feel my head becoming clear and light. There was no IV connected to her, and she had no bandages. She actually looked well, aside from how pale her skin was.

"Are you doing okay?" I asked.

"How are you feeling?" Jessica asked at the same time.

Montana inhaled a deep breath and her eyes squinted. "I'm good." She paused and then gritted her teeth. "Thank you."

I gave Jessica a look, and she gave me the same one right back. We were thinking the same thing: Montana was obviously still in pain. I glanced at Jessica and wondered if she was using her gifts, but as I stared more intensely at her and began to sense her, it seemed that she was not. She was just as confused as I was.

We sat in chairs near Montana's bed. I sat in the one closest to her to see if I could sense her, although I doubted I would be able to.

"Do you feel any pain?" I asked.

She smiled at me pleasantly. "No, I'm fine. How are you guys?"

I sat back in the chair, defeated, and glanced at Jessica, who raised her eyebrows as if to say, "*My turn.*"

She sat forward in her chair and leaned in closer to Montana. "We're good, thanks. What did the doctor say?"

Montana pushed herself up in the bed, but then stopped suddenly, shaking her head slightly. Her eyes squinted with the same painful expression, but only for a second before she composed herself.

"I'm fine, guys," she said with a smile. "Really, I'm good. Please don't ask me again, okay?"

Jessica and I looked at each other, our eyes communicating confusion and concern.

"Okay," we said, nodding our heads. "Okay."

∞

We stayed there until nightfall, talking and laughing. Several times, the nurse had to come in to tell us to keep our voices down, and she finally ended up kicking us out. We said our goodbyes and left the hospital.

"Jess, can I ask you something?" I asked softly as we walked through the parking garage.

There was a long silence. She walked with her eyes focused on the ground.

"Yeah," she finally answered.

"It wasn't you making her relaxed?"

Her laugh echoed throughout the garage, making it sound much more thunderous. "I think you and I both know that answer."

"I can't sense her, Jess." She stopped and turned to look at me. "Her expressions tell me more than my gifts do," I admitted softly.

"I don't know what to tell you, lady," she said, walking over to her car. I followed. "Are you really worried about this?" she asked as we slid into our seats.

"Should I be?" I asked, shrugging. "I don't know—it's just . . ." I paused, trying to find the right words. "I think she makes me question myself, my gifts. That's never happened before. Not from a God or Goddess, let alone a mortal." I paused again, prefacing my last and final thought. "*Is* she mortal?"

Jessica laughed loudly. "Yes, silly. Why wouldn't she be?"

"I don't know," I said, shrugging again.

"Well, don't worry too much about it," she told me.

Giving her a sideways glance, I reminded her, "I don't know how to worry." I turned away, staring out the window. "But I guess you're right."

That was the first and last time I verbalized my thoughts about Montana's mortality.

Chapter 10

Apria Doves

Halfway through November, I still hadn't contacted my family or friends. Between classes, writing papers, and moving into the new house with Britta, Jaden, and Diane, things on Earth had been keeping me very busy. Even when Thanksgiving break came and I had time off, I was still entertaining thoughts of not returning home for a visit. Was I avoiding my loved ones for some reason I did not consciously understand?

Everyone but Britta and I had already gone home for the holiday. I leaned against her bedroom door as I watched her patiently squeeze her suitcase shut and struggle to zip it closed, then followed her outside. She shoved the oversized suitcase into her car and slammed the hatchback shut. "Okay, that's it, I think," she said, a bit out of breath.

After we hugged goodbye, she climbed into her car and left, waving as she reversed down the driveway. As I watched her disappear down the street, a giant brown leaf fell delicately from overhead, teetering gently back and forth until it finally kissed the pavement, joining the family of leaves that had previously followed the same ritual. A very strange feeling came to me as I stared at the leaves—as if something was missing.

"Hey, Brosi!" I looked up to see Montana strolling up the sidewalk, waving to me.

The hospital had released her a couple days before, telling her to rest up and take things easy. For a long time after, none of us would know what had really happened to her. At the time, all I knew was that it had something to do with her chest and she'd had a lot of x-rays done. She said she felt great, but she still seemed in pain sometimes.

As she got closer, I noticed her hood was arranged on the side of her neck again.

"I wanted to say goodbye to you guys," she said with a big smile.

"You missed Britta," I told her.

"Oh," she said, shrugging.

Her presence on campus surprised me. After her injury, I'd thought her parents would want her to come home immediately.

"So when are you leaving?" I asked. "Do you need help packing?"

"No," she said calmly, her eyes landing on the same leaves I'd been staring at. I thought she would say more, but there was a long silence before she lifted her head and caught me staring. "I mean . . . no, thank you. I'm not—I can't go home."

"Why not?" I asked.

She beckoned me to walk with her down the street. "I can't leave because the doctors want me to come in for another checkup after Thanksgiving." She kicked a rock in front of her. "My mom and I decided it would be pointless for me to go home."

I nodded. "So you're going to stay in your dorm?"

She looked at me a bit confused, and then bit her lip as if I was aggravating her. It was probably hard for her to be away from her family. I had noticed she seemed to be very close to them; she talked to her mom on the phone nearly every day.

"I have nowhere else to go," she finally said, kicking the rock again.

It was a sad truth. I thought about taking her with me, picturing her reaction as we ascended through the clouds to my home in the Heavens.

"So when are *you* leaving?" I heard her ask, snapping me out of my trance.

"I don't think I am," I said, surprising myself. I hadn't really decided until that moment whether to stay or go.

From the corner of my eye, I saw her slow down and look at me. "Why?" she asked, the tone of her voice admonishing.

"I'm not sure."

"Well, what do your parents say?"

I looked at her. "I don't know."

"You haven't talked to them?" she scolded in an even harsher tone.

I shook my head, and she looked at me like I had grown an extra head.

"Okay," I told her. "I'll talk to them."

She smiled instantly and beckoned me to keep walking with her. "Call them right now on the way to the market."

I pulled out my phone and saw I had missed a call and a voicemail. Lifting the phone to my ear, I gulped when I heard my mother's frazzled voice and *felt* her distress wash over me. Her words quivered, and she seemed on the verge of tears as she asked, *"Where have you been? Are you okay?"*

I didn't know what I would tell her because there was no good excuse as to why I hadn't been in contact. I bit my lip and tried to keep a stoic face in front of Montana, who was now eying me.

"It's my mom," I whispered. She nodded, keeping her gaze focused on me.

Then my father came on the line. "Petra, John's not doing so well. Perhaps you can come home and talk to him. We hope to hear from you." The message ended, and I slowly put my phone back into my pocket.

"Are you okay?" she asked.

I stared back at her blankly, wondering what I should do. Something had been going on with John all the while I had been on Earth.

47

Am I okay? How do people feel in situations like this?

"Yes," I finally told her. "I'm hungry—let's go."

∞

It took us much longer returning from the market than it did getting there because Montana struggled on the way back. The delay didn't bother me, but Montana seemed agitated. She would try to walk fast but then slow down, grabbing her chest. When that happened, I would slow my pace too, hoping to prevent her from thinking she needed to move faster. She generally ignored me, though, and kept trying to speed up her pace. It would have been quite comedic if I hadn't been so concerned.

"Are you in a hurry?" I finally asked.

She swung her head in my direction, looking both surprised and angry at me for interrupting her concentration. "No. Why?"

My lips eased into a smile. "It seems like you're in a rush."

"Well, I'm not."

"Good." I smiled again. "Because it's nice out tonight, and I want to enjoy it."

She nodded in agreement, and we both looked up at the purple and blue sky. An easy, chilly breeze blew every so often. It was just right, though—not too cold.

We reached her townhouse, and I held the bags of food—along with the two bottles of wine she'd insisted we buy—as she juggled for her keys.

Back at the market was the first time I'd heard her speak of her sister. She'd shown me her sister's driver's license before grabbing two red wines—from the cheapest selection—and our favorite cinnamon bread.

"So do you have any other siblings?" I asked now.

"Just my older sister," she said.

I reclined back on the couch and waited for her to say more, but instead she sat staring at the ground, grinning from whatever memory was playing in her head. After her moment, she walked over, grabbed one of the wine bottles, and placed it on the wooden table in front of me. She grinned at me and started to open the bottle. She struggled a bit—the bottle nearly flew from her fingers, and she barely caught it before it fell over.

I giggled to myself. "So what are you going to do tomorrow?"

Her face was serious as she poured the wine into a blue plastic cup. "I don't know. My mom's friend lives in Colorado Springs, so I guess I'll be going there."

"Well, good," I said. "I'm glad."

"Glad for what?" She stopped pouring, waiting anxiously for my answer.

"I'm glad you won't be alone for the holiday."

She pondered my answer for a bit, then blinked and shook off whatever she was thinking. She finished pouring for herself and then handed me the half-empty bottle. "Here, finish it."

I looked at her, and then at the bottle, before draining most of it. The wine reminded me of Dion. Wine was his weapon of choice—he took it wherever he went, like a power source for his gifts, which had always been strong, just like those of his great ancestor, Dionysus. We had all seen them abundantly displayed during the Ten-Day Celebration and other Heavenly festivities. Dion's life was a massive party; I didn't think he had a serious bone in his body.

I smiled, thinking of him. He always made an entrance—glowing marble-white teeth, light mahogany skin, unruly brown curly hair sticking out in every direction as if he had just had sex, which was usually the case. His chic style and boundless charm hypnotized all the great Deities.

Montana reached for her blue cup and snagged a slice of cinnamon bread. "I can't help but notice how Jess talks about you like she knows you from before."

The piece of cinnamon bread I had just swallowed caught in the back of my throat. "Oh. She really doesn't," I choked out, "but she knew one of my best friends from back home."

"Oh really? From Texas?"

I shrugged and stuffed a big piece of cinnamon bread in my mouth. "This bread is so good," I said, my mouth full, praying I hadn't made it too obvious that I didn't want to answer her question. I was trying to be as vague as possible without telling a lie. "What part of Montana are you from again?"

She leaned back into the couch, giving me a smile. More than a few awkward seconds went by before she answered.

"I don't think I ever told you," she pondered, smiling, "but I'm from Hobson."

My face dropped at the word—Hobson, the same town where Titanus was secretly built.

She continued talking, seemingly oblivious to my reaction. "It's a tiny town. I doubt you've heard of it."

"N-No . . . I've heard of it," I told her, and she smiled at me. "How are you feeling by the way?"
She shot me a look before taking a sip from her cup. "I'm good . . . it's all good." She looked up at me. "Please stop asking?"

I gave a slight smile and nodded, then took a long drag from the bottle. She then slowly reached toward the table, grabbed my phone, and began scrolling through it. "You only have one number saved."

"I only need one."

She shot me a sarcastic smile and started typing, smiling as she did so, then handed the phone back to me, grinning. "Now you have two."

On the screen, I saw the phone number and her name—Taylor Montana Letto.

"And when you're bored," she said, "you can text me."

49

I laughed at the fact that she knew the secret nickname I had given her. I'd never used it out loud nor told anyone about it. "Thanks, but I don't even know how to text."

She laughed, almost spilling on herself. "Here, I'll show you." She reached for her phone and started typing. Her fingers moved so fast. "There. Just wait a second."

My phone beeped, and she got up from her couch to plop herself near me. "See? Now click to open it."

I did as she instructed and read aloud what she had sent: *"I'm glad you're here."* I looked up at her and chuckled quietly. "Me too."

She smiled back. In that smile, I saw something, felt something. Was it from her?

"Now you're supposed to text me back," she explained, then giggled. "Do you know how to do that?"

"Um, no."

She leaned in closer. I sat still, waiting to see what she was going to do. I could smell the wine on her lips and tongue. She sat just as still as I did, and for a second, I wondered if she was still there. I looked up and found myself at eye level with her lips. Gently, she reached over, softly untangling the phone from my fingers, and started to text while holding the phone out so I could see what she was doing.
"You see, it's just like a keyboard," she said, showing me. "And then you press send."

I nodded, took the phone from her, and began composing a text. After I finished, I sent it and then looked up, waiting to hear her phone go off. It buzzed softly in her hand. She casually picked it up and looked at the screen. She laughed, reading my text aloud: *"I wanted to make sure you were okay."* She looked up and grinned brightly at me. "I don't need a babysitter."

The words propelled me back in time. Eva had said the same thing to me after nearly entering Tartarus. *"I don't need a babysitter, Petra,"* she'd said, but I could sense her dwindling hope and depression.

Tartarus was a horrendous place, a dungeon where Deities were tormented for eternity. It was like Hades, but much farther below the Earth and darker, and with more suffering. It was the place Deities were sent after doing something unforgivable.
Eva's lover was sent there after attempting to release Cronus from Tartarus. In doing so, he had hoped to receive Cronus 'powers. Eva had followed him, hoping to convince him not to do it. Instead, he nearly convinced her to join him. It was a desperate chase, but my father and I had been able to find her before she had completely entered Tartarus.

I watched every tear fall from her eyes as we waited for The Moirai to seal her lover's fate. After that, we never saw him again. I "babysat" her for decades, and I experienced the suffering of Tartarus vicariously by looking into Eva's burning eyes every day and feeling every piece of her heart shatter.

"I should go," I said suddenly, snapping back to the present. I rose, stumbling over the wooden table and knocking the empty bottle on the floor. Montana bolted upright in the same dizzy manner but managed to hold herself up.

"You know you can stay the night if you need to," she said.

" No, no," I said, lurching to the door. "But hey, text me," I said, laughing at my own joke.

She wrapped her arms around my shoulders, squeezing so tightly I was scared she was going to hurt herself.

"Thanks for letting me stay, Tay. Ha, that rhymed," I said, laughing, realizing I was tipsier than I thought. I gave one last goodbye and headed out the door, walking down the steps and into the chilly air.

I looked up into the sky and saw the stars. With a drunken slur, I managed to say "Home," out loud to the sky, and then I sat myself down on the curb and cradled my chin in my hands. "I miss home," I said, and then looked back up to the sky.

And I miss Dion and Apria, was what I thought right before one star began to shine brighter than the others in the sky. I squinted to see as the light began to grow, and as it got closer I noticed it was not a bright star, but a white dove. It was a bit larger than normal doves, and it grew as it approached. I was hypnotized by its beauty. A sudden glow then brightened the dark sky, looking like a moon being born. And then, just as suddenly, Apria dropped to the ground right in front of me.

Before my eyes could adjust, Apria's arms were around my neck.

"Petra," she said softly. I could almost feel her words caress my skin.

I blinked a couple of times, still trying to adjust my eyes. I could not believe she was in front of me, and on Earth.

"Apria, how did you do that?"

"Do what?" she asked.

"How did you descend as a dove?"

She laughed loudly, still glowing brightly after her descending transformation.

"You're glowing."

She looked down at herself and frowned. "We should go. We might cause a scene."

"No, Apria, *you* might cause a scene," I joked.

Her lips curled into a smile, and her arms swung around me again. "I've missed you, Petra." She let go of me quickly. "Hurry, though, we must go."

With those words, I suddenly found myself on the transporter. Up and up we went, higher into the stars. I wasn't paying attention to our direction, knowing Apria was guiding us. Not until we landed did I realize we were somewhere unfamiliar—a forest I had never seen before. A large blue moon was shining above, casting the most beautiful bluish-grey tint on the trees, giving the forest a deep blue hue.

As Apria and I entered the forest, she began searching—for what, I had no idea. She glowed brightly as she led me farther in. Finally, she stopped and turned around to smile at me. A powerful shriek coursed through my body. It was not coming from Apria, but from behind me. I turned and felt its warmth instantly. Several feet away stood a huge, magnificent fox.

Chapter 11

Dion Vindé

The gigantic fox stood proudly on all fours. Its fur was a rainbow of browns and reds, the coat falling delicately over its muscular build. Its ears pointed high above its piercing black eyes, and its teeth were bared—not in a growl, but as if the creature were actually smiling at me.

Apria stood still, smiling back at the fox. In a sudden move, it made a dash, heading right toward me.

I couldn't move. My feet wanted to run, but my eyes remained fixed on the fox's beauty. Closer and closer it came, and I could sense its excitement. Within inches of me, the fox suddenly transformed, tackling me hard to the ground. I opened my eyes to Dion's smile. Immediately, I swung my arms tightly around him.

"You didn't miss me at all now, did you?" he asked sarcastically.

I shoved him off me. "Well, look who it is—the forever famous Dion Vindé!" My grin faded. I had never witnessed gifts of transformation from my two best friends before, and yet now I had seen both of them morph in the same night. I looked at them quizzically.

"How did you do that?"

They looked at each other and threw their heads back in laughter.

"A lot has changed in the past few months," Apria said, glancing at Dion.

"Is that so?" I asked.

Dion pulled himself up from the forest floor and casually dusted himself off. He threw his arm over my shoulders, tucking me close to him, and moved us even deeper into the foggy blue forest, which was not dark as I'd first thought. Between the oversized moon hanging above the tall pines and the glow from Dion and Apria, it was actually very well lit. I looked at them, at their glow that was much brighter than mine.

"Why aren't I glowing anymore?" I asked.

They stopped. Dion detached his arm from me and stepped back beside Apria. Both of them scrutinized me, tilting their heads.

"You are . . . a little," Apria said reassuringly.

"No, it's definitely faded. Weird," Dion added, negating Apria's attempt to put my mind at ease.

"Well, what does that mean?"

Dion looked at Apria, formulating a thought. "Doesn't it mean there's a change occurring?" he asked, still looking at Apria.

I sensed his worry the instant the words came out of his mouth.

"Y–yeah, I think. It's not a good change. At least that's what they say." Her voice cracked—also not a good sign.

"Who says?" I questioned, trying to ignore their troubled emotions.

There was a long silence, silence that seemed to fill in the spaces between the trees. I stood patiently, waiting for one of them to speak, but they just kept exchanging glances, neither wanting to go first. A great swell of fear pressed against my chest and nipped at my nose.

"What are you guys so scared to tell me?" I finally asked.

Dion threw his hands up. "We're so damn easy to sense!"

"It's okay," Apria told him. "We just need help."

"What are you guys talking about? And how did you transform?"

Apria finally stepped forward, putting her arm around me and hugging me close. I could feel her better when she touched me and had to wonder if she was doing it on purpose.

"There's this new kind of training at Titanus," she said. "The professors are teaching us how *not* to feel. How to control our emotions and not let them be seen or sensed."

As she spoke, I began sensing her despair—and her hope.

"You see, Pei," Dion said. He paused to look at Apria guiltily, and Apria rolled her eyes slightly before he continued. "We sort of need you." He stopped again, and I could feel his restraint.

Apria noticed and took over. "Petra, you need to come to Titanus and share your gifts with us and the young ones. You aren't helping yourself by attending an all-mortal school on Earth." She took a deep breath. "You need to share with us how to sense emotion and how to not feel."

I must have still been tipsy because I could not have imagined that what they were asking of me was real.

"Why would any Deity want my gift?" My voice was a whisper.

Dion stepped closer, towering over me. "Because having emotions is the only thing that is keeping us from being great Gods like the Titans."

My theory about the Titans' power was quite different from theirs. I didn't believe the Titans were powerful because they felt nothing, but rather, because they didn't understand the potential strength of their emotions. Because their power was too overwhelming for any emotion to be felt, it ruined them. I was finally beginning to understand why some of us tried to live with the mortals.

My mother, of course, had been right all along. Knowing how to feel like the mortals—with all their emotional variations and everyday highs and lows—would balance out our powers. If the Gods became too strong like the Titans had, our power would disable us from feeling the most important emotions of all—unconditional love and mercy. I knew this even without being able to feel. Never had I felt mercy or unconditional love, and yet I knew their power could change things immensely.

"Isn't that a good thing?" I asked. My voice was still low, and my words were like bullets from a shotgun. "The Titans were horrible Deities. The things they did were ghastly. Even Zeus didn't want to be like them." I shook my head. "You guys, mortals keep us humane. That is why I'm at this school. I'm learning that having *feelings* is what stops us from being like the Titans, and that's a good thing."

I sat down on the forest floor and leaned back against a tree trunk.

Dion seated himself next to me. "Pei, please think about it, okay?" I thought I already had.

"You can save many Deities, including your family."

My eyes widened, and a flash of my brother crying at Point Dume entered my mind. "John," I whispered, letting his name slip from my tongue.

"Yes, Pei, this can help him—before it's too late."

I narrowed my eyes at Dion. "What do you mean before it's too late?"

"Have you not talked to your mom or dad?" he asked quietly.

I did not answer him, but instead kept staring, waiting for him to answer my question. Dion looked worriedly at Apria, who wore the same concerned expression as he did.

Apria knelt in front of me, taking my hands. "Your brother is not doing well at all, Petra," she said tenderly, trying not to alarm me.

"I suppose it takes a while to get over an old lover," I said, my voice even.

They looked at each other again with that same guilty, nervous stare.

The moonlight shone through a space between the trees and bathed us in a blue sheen. That was when I saw the healing tissue on Dion's inner forearm. He had been branded. I looked closer and instantly recognized what it was: the Greek letter λ. Everyone in the Heavens knew what that meant. It was the symbol of the Lambdas—a forsaken cult, a brotherhood—and only the Enlightened were branded with it. The brand represented a bond, an understanding. But it separated the branded from all other Deities. It was not something to be proud of, nor to display publicly.

"Dion, is that . . ."

He followed my gaze to his forearm and gently covered it with his hand, as if it were an open wound. "Yes," he said softly. "That is what I have been trying to tell you, Pei. . . This," he slightly uncovered the brand. "All because of these damn *feelings*."

I closed my eyes and tilted my head back against the tree, picturing myself on my make-believe island, a place I always dreamed about when I wanted some alone time. I would envision myself lying on the beach, gazing out over the clear ocean waters, sand between my toes and the smell of the sea filling my nose. It was my own Heaven, my own paradise. I opened my eyes and smiled peacefully.

"Dion," I asked. "What are you going to do? Why have you decided this?"

He inched closer to me. "I did not decide. I did not *want* to feel this way, but I literally. . . literally cannot help it. It's like an epidemic has spread in the Heavens, Pei. More and more Deities have become branded, causing them to turn to suicide." He paused, and I saw the tears building up in the corners of his eyes.

I had never seen Dion like this, and I waited until I felt him regain control. When he did, he continued, "I did not choose this," he said through gritted teeth. "I just fell in love, and next thing I know, I'm branded."

I took a deep breath. "You guys, I can't help you—at least not until I graduate from this mortal school. I can't just leave. I'm on specific orders from my parents. You both know who my father is. There is no way I can defy him."

Dion eased his head back against the pine, and Apria stood up, crossing her arms. I felt their hopes dashed to the ground, falling quicker than rain.

"Pei, they're threatening to kick me out of school if they catch any sign of 'Lambda activity.'"

Lambda activity?" What makes you so sure I can save you and the other young Deities with my gifts?"

He shrugged. "Because, aside from suicide, you're the only antidote we could think of," he said, his voice still unusually soft and low.

"Why can't the Elders help? Isn't there any way for you to save—"

"They've been trying for centuries, Petra," Apria cut in angrily.

"Well, why didn't we know about this before?" I asked. I sat up and stared hard at her.

"I don't know, but emotions have become such a problem that the Elders informed our professors at Titanus that they must start training us not to feel," she said solemnly.

"Out of all of the thousands of Gods and Goddesses, Petra, you are the only one we know of who has the gift of no emotion," Dion added.

I listened to them, heard everything they said, and yet still could not believe a word of it. It didn't seem real to me. We were invincible, weren't we?

I shook my head. "I can't," I told them once more. "Until, my schooling ends, the professors will have to think of another way."

Chapter 12

Another Sleepless Night

I could not stop thinking about what was happening in the Heavens and the request Dion and Apria had made of me. In fact, those thoughts were all that filled my head. I lost a lot of sleep thinking about why our Elders would conclude it was best for us not to feel. What would no feelings resolve?

When my phone vibrated under my pillow at two in the morning, I looked at the screen through one eye, trying to focus on the name. I should have guessed it would be Montana—this was the fourth time this week she had texted me at this hour.

"Hey, are you awake?"

"Of course I am. Can't sleep again?" I texted back.

"Yeah, you too?"

"Yup."

It was the first week of December and absolutely freezing at night. Our heater didn't work, so sometimes it seemed even colder in the house than it was outside. I saw my breath cloud in front of me as I exhaled.

"Question game?" the next text read. I laughed.

"Of course. You go first." "What is your biggest fear?"

I stared at the screen for quite some time, and then put my phone down to really consider the question.

"I don't know," I wrote after a while. "I suppose nothing. What's your best memory?"

"Nothing? Interesting. My best memory is going berry picking with my mom. What's your favorite song right now?"

That was an easy question. There were many songs I liked, but there was one in particular that never got old to me.

"'The Nicest Thing' by Kate Nash." "I've never heard of it."

"It's a good song."

"I bet," she texted. "It's probably another sad song. You do love your sad songs. Well, I'm going to bed. Good night, Dismal."

I giggled again. *"Okay, goodnight."*

I put my phone on the end table and caught the time on the clock. 3:33. So late, and I still had no hope of falling asleep. I lay there a little longer until I decided I should do something productive with my thoughts.

I flipped on a light, grabbed my folder from my backpack and found a pen on my end table. Plopping back onto my bed, I began flipping through my notes from Dr.
Griffin's class. They were nowhere near legible, nor did they make any sense. In fact, what I had written had nothing to do with his class. It was all just scribbles of my thoughts, scattered and incomplete. I flipped the page and saw that I had composed a poem of sorts that I had no recollection of even writing.

I am neither gorgeous nor ugly. I am neither tall nor short.
I am not strong nor weak. I am not smart nor dumb.
I am not perfect nor flawed.

I am not serious nor a joke. You cannot love me but you cannot hate me.
I do not do right nor do I do wrong. I cannot love but can never hate.
I am the best and yet, the worst.

I am hard to be around, but impossible to ignore. You can neither be with me nor can you be without.
I am the effect but also the cause.

I am the everything in between.
The average equalizer.
I am who I am.

I sat staring at the poem. I didn't understand it, nor why I had written it. What subconscious state had I been in to bring that out?

Without thinking more about it, I flipped the page and began to write.

I am lost. I must be . . .
No words could express my mind any further than I could see.
I used to be able to talk about
life for hours, and be proud of
who I was, and my powers.

Gods, have you forgotten me?
How did I end up here without thee?
This was not where I even wanted to be.

Was this on purpose
to help me? Or was
this your trick of
mockery?

Unlike myself . . .

59

I do not know how to act like myself anymore.
I lost myself while
trying to soar. Dear
life, please get under
control, and find the
path you were on
before.

The river is
heavily flowing,
and the road is
crazily winding.
Gods hold me down,
and let me ride it peacefully

Can I trust thee? (I do not even know how to trust.) Can I find someone
real? (I do not even know what real is.) Would I then begin to feel?
Or would they have come and gone for me to miss?

Gods, are you there?
I come knocking at your doors. Do you care?
I know this happens plenty.
Can't I just find me and be
me proudly? And not care
if they judge too harshly?
Will they love the true me?
The me that has been made from thee?

Why can I not feel?
Why hast thou made me without that
gene? Alone I will be then; fall asleep,
and awake, forever searching for the
piece that will never fit.
Will somebody fix me?

Chapter 13

Winter Break

As the days got colder, Britta grew increasingly more difficult to be around. Her overwhelming emotions were endless, spilling out of her every day and ranging from the sun's warmth to Antarctic blasts of cold.

Back at home in the Heavens, they'd be getting ready for our Ten-Day Celebration. Every year before the New Year, we counted down with ten days of dining on the finest wine and cheeses, music and dancing in the streets, and a different gaming event every day. The games included boxing, archery, pankration, and our Pentathlon—discus and javelin throwing, long jump, wrestling, and a foot race.

I was postponing my trip home as long as I could. Although home would be a lot warmer, the thought of the pressure I would feel from my family's worry made enduring Britta's emotions a bit more bearable. For the time being, I was content to remain on Earth.

It was Sunday, and the best Christmas movies were playing on television. Jaden sat with me, cuddled in her blanket and absorbed in her phone.

"Are you still texting him?" I asked, grinning in anticipation of her response.

She smiled back guiltily.

"Is he coming over after Christmas for your New Year's party?"

She smiled again. "Yes! And he's bringing a couple of friends as well." She nodded at me, implying that one of them would be for me.

"Oh goody," I said sarcastically, and then smiled.

Just then, Britta stomped into the living room, her boyfriend treading lightly behind her. They must have been fighting again. Jaden and I exchanged a quick glance, each of us giving the other an exasperated look that said, *"Here we go again!"*

"Alan, you are *not* going," she insisted harshly.

"Why? It's his birthday!"

"I don't care. You drove up here to see *me*, and we're going to spend the whole day together."

Alan's sigh expressed pure hopelessness. He shut his mouth and didn't say anything more.

Jaden and I looked at each other once again, probably thinking the same thing, and we both shook our heads, laughing. Poor Alan seemed to lose every fight.

"What are you guys laughing at?"

I looked up to see Britta's infuriated face. There was a pressure on my neck, as if she had her hands gripped around it. Jaden stopped laughing immediately and focused on her phone again, ignoring Britta. I looked at Jaden, chuckled at her cowardice, and then felt that same angry grip on my neck again, even stronger this time. Britta glared at me.

"Sorry, Britta," I said.

I stood up, walked into the kitchen to put my cup in the sink, and returned to the couch. Britta's eyes didn't leave me once, watching me every step of the way. I could feel her stare as I went back to watching television.

"You think you're perfect, don't you?"

For a second, I thought the voice was in my head. Then I looked up and saw Britta was still staring at me. I took a peek at Jaden and saw her sitting there wide-eyed with her mouth open. That was when I knew I hadn't been hearing things.

"Excuse me?" I asked.

She moved toward me and stopped at the sofa, standing over me, pointing. "You are the fakest person I have ever met!" she yelled, and her words seemed to consume the entire living room. "You sit on your high horse, and you think you're so special."

Questions ran through my head: *Is this real? Does she know who I am?* How could she, when I had lived with her less than a couple months? *Can she see right through me? Am I fake?*

I guess in a way I was. I was trying to live in a world I didn't like—a world for mortals—but I was just trying my best to fit in.

I sat quietly, and I could feel her getting nervous. I looked up into her burning blue eyes, tilting my head, and asked with all the confusion I could muster, "Where did this come from?"

"You walk around here, Petra, all cocky with your head held so high!"

She said this like it was a bad thing to be proud of yourself. That was how everyone in the Heavens was. *Shouldn't everyone—mortals and Deities—be proud and confident?*

I consulted Jaden to see if she was hearing what I was hearing. She was as motionless as I was, her mouth still open, and her eyes even wider than before. I could barely sense her because Britta's emotions were so overbearing. I tried to sort through Britta's cloud of emotions—anger, hurt, fear . . . jealousy. *Jealousy? What does she have to be jealous about?*

"Why don't you say something?" she yelled into my face. "Look at you trying to be perfect and hide how mad you are right now!" She gave me a final glare before snatching Alan's hand and stomping back down the hall to her bedroom, slamming the door behind her.

I sat there, wishing she was right. I *wished* I was hiding how angry I was. I wished I felt anger enough to want to hide it. But as usual, I didn't feel anything. And once again, someone was hurt because of it.

I looked back at Jaden. She had tears in her soft green eyes, as if she was the one who'd been yelled at.

I chuckled softly. "Why are you crying?"

She wiped a tear from beneath her eyelashes and one from her nose before speaking. "That was the meanest thing I've ever seen," she finally said. "Why didn't you stand up for yourself?"

I didn't understand. "Why would I need to stand up for myself? She was obviously angry at something else before she turned on me."

"But she didn't need to say those things. That was so messed up."

"Well, are they true? Do you believe what she says?" I asked.

"No!" she blurted, and then paused, as if collecting her thoughts. "I mean, you are a bit too confident," she said, scrunching up her face as if bracing for an angry outburst from me.

I laughed at how funny she looked. "I must say, I find that odd. But I can't say she's wrong. She must see something in me that I cannot."

Jaden's tilted head made me wonder if she was asking the same question I was: *How confident am I?*

∞

Colorado was beautiful in its garb of white. Snow dusted its trees and forest floors, as white fog hung suspended around the mountains, protecting and hiding everything. As I soared up to the Heavens and looked down to Earth, the white haze below the glass floor at my feet fogged up like a puff of breath on a car window.

The fog got too thick to see anything through the Heavens' glass floor, so I sat there, staring at it, not through it. Was I like that glass? I too had thick fog preventing anyone from seeing through me. Would something, or someone clear the fog? Only time would tell.

It was the 24th of December, the day before Christmas. In the Heavens, there was no such holiday. We had the Ten-Day Celebration, and we were in the midst of it as I arrived to the Heavens. I missed two days of it, and I was already hearing all the crazy stories that have been happening. For any celebration in the Heavens, Gods and Goddesses come from all over, and I wondered if I would see Ricky during the festivities. I was excited to see friends I hadn't seen since leaving Gaianus, and of course Apria and Dion, who would soon be meeting up with me.

My father and mother had already taken seats in one of the tower balconies overlooking the celebration in the streets, and I assumed my brother and sister were there as well.

"You ready to go?" Dion said behind me.

I turned around and smiled. He grabbed my arm gently and picked me up, giving me the biggest hug. Releasing me, he adjusted his white sarong and purple belt and fussed with the purple-flowered wreath on his head, tilting it to one side. He then looked me up and down.

"You look stunning!"

I wore a traditional white toga with a V-neck that plunged down my chest. Green and gold ribbon decorated the sides and collar, matching my green and gold wreath and belt. Chandelier earrings of white gold and diamonds dangled from my ears. The gold sandals on my feet wrapped around to the top of my calves with green ribbon.

Apria walked toward us. She wore a white satin toga that tied tightly around her waist and cut down her chest in a heart shape. Rose gold jewelry adorned her arms, fingers, and ankles. Her wreath of roses had a rose gold lining that circled the top of her head, and her toga was long, draping below the luminescent flooring. She was graceful as she made her way toward me, leaned in, and kissed me on the cheek.

"It's good to see you again, Petra."

"You as well," I said, returning her cheek kisses.

"So how has training been going?" I asked them as we made our way toward Via Olympia, the main street in Mount Olympus.

Apria wrapped her arm around mine as we walked.

"Well," she began, but then hesitated, holding something back. I leaned away from her, biting my lip. She was really fighting herself. I looked at Dion—he was focused on the road ahead, his expression serious.

"We wanted to tell you about this one class we had on Ancient Greek history. We dug deep into the history of our ancestors—back to the time of Ouranos and Gaia and the Twelve Titans—"

"I mean, Pei, we were literally reading books I don't think anyone has seen before," Dion cut in excitedly.

"They were more like tablets," Apria added.

"Tablets, scrolls, carvings—you name it. And only Titanus had these archives."

"We started from the time of Ouranos and Gaia," Dion continued, "and went through the Twelve Titans and then to the overthrow of the Titans after the Titanomachy—"

"But everyone in the Heavens—and on Earth—knows about the Titanomachy," I told them.

Titanomachy was just a fancy word for the Titan War between the twelve ruling Titans and the young Olympian Gods and Goddesses. It happened way before my existence, about 200,000 Earth years ago. After ten long years of war, Zeus and the Twelve Olympians finally overthrew the Twelve Titans. Zeus then sent the Titan fighters, including Cronus, who was their leader, to Tartarus. Some Titans—like Oceanus, the God of all the oceans—were not sent to Tartarus because they hadn't cared to fight in the war.

"Yes," Dion said, "but we were taught the real reason for the war. It may be a different story Gaianus has been telling." He eyed Apria again, and this time I could feel their tension.

We had almost reached our destination, and I could see the huge marble pillars from which hung the gigantic *Via Olympia* sign. We stopped before entering, and Apria held me back with her arm; I felt her worry fall around me.

"What's wrong?" I asked.

"Before you see your family, we want to give you some news that your sister told me last night." I could read only surprise in Apria's sapphire eyes. "Yes?" I questioned, intrigued.

"Your brother and sister. . ." she began cautiously.

"They are to be transferred to Titanus this upcoming semester," Dion added, just as cautiously.

"Okay…" I was hesitant, knowing this was leading somewhere. I should have felt their excitement, their happiness, but all I felt was something heavy. They looked at each other again. By now I had noticed that every time that happened, it meant something not good.

"Along with everyone else at Gaianus," Dion said, finally.

I paused to feel them before responding. They were waiting for something—my reaction, I was guessing.

"There will be no more Gaianus training school. They are closing it," Apria concluded.

Thoughts spun through my head like a pinwheel. What was going on, and why?

"That's … interesting," I muttered.

Dion and Apria looked at each other and blinked, and then turned back to me.

"Petra," Dion said. "Something is happening. Things are happening. For Gaianus to close . . ." He paused and took a breath. "We should prepare for anything."

"You need to be here—with us," Apria added, sounding sad, "with your kind. For the Gods 'sake, Petra, you do not even know who your ancestors are or where you came from or how you got your gifts—or anything." Her voice broke off softly. And then it returned, just as gentle. "You don't know who you are, Petra, and you don't know what is happening in the Heavens."

The words struck me heavily with the truth, and I reeled back. I wanted to say something and tried but couldn't get the words out. Instead, I left them and headed through the entrance and into the celebration. Before diving into the crowd, I stopped to scan the miles of toga-wearing Gods and Goddesses. Everything was so beautiful. Rose petals and confetti fell continuously, and the street was blanketed in festive décor. Streamers, balloons, and flashing lights filled the pink sky. Platters of bread, cheese, and fruit were being served, and gallons of wine being poured into chalices, half of it spilling onto the glass pavement. Deities were laughing, hugging, and kissing each other, complementing one another on their attire.

65

Some wore hoods and sashes, others tunics with caps or sarongs. All were accented with tons of jewelry.

Some Gods dripped with diamonds and gold and some chose pieces that were simple yet elegant. All were styled according to one's character and personal taste, but one thing was the same—the wreaths we all wore on our heads.

The color of the wreath indicated the type of gift passed down to the Diety from their ancestors. Apria, John, and other Gods and Goddesses of Love and Beauty wore red. Dion and the other Draconian and Bacchus Deities wore purple. Blue was for the Athlete, Warrior, and Hunter Gods and Goddesses. My sister wore silver—representing the Wise, the Artists, the Poets and the Musicians.

Lastly, there was green—worn by the Nurtured and the Others. The Nurtured were mortals who had risen above the immortals 'expectations and been allowed to drink from the Styx River to become immortal themselves. My parents wore green, for my father had once been a great mortal warrior, and he had taken my mother as his eternal companion. The Others were those of us who didn't fit into any other category.

"Dion, don't forget to—" I heard Apria say as they came up beside me.

"I know, I know," Dion said lightly, wrapping a long vine around his forearm to cover his Lambda brand as if he'd had a lot of practice doing so. Apria watched over him, and I scanned the crowd to see if anyone was watching.

When it was done, the three of us walked side by side down Via Olympia, observing the crowd of white robes. Dion pulled three small kotsifali grapes out from under his sarong. Their high alcohol content could be overwhelming, but they tasted sweet like candy. We ate them as we merged into the crowd, joining in the festivities.

I soon spotted my long-time friend Chandra. Her long, dark, curly hair made her stand out anywhere. As I got closer, I saw that she was with a couple of other Gaianus classmates, Christy Lotis and Ann Hest. I rushed up from behind to surprise them, but they had already spotted me.

"*Brosi!*" the three sang in unison.

"How are you guys?" I shouted back, trying to make my voice heard over the loud celebration behind me.

"We've missed you!" Christy said, flashing a fetching smile. Her bronze eyes twinkled like glitter, and her long, abundant curls fell gracefully over her satiny mahogany skin. "You have a lot to tell us, we hear."

"Yes, she does," Chandra said, dark curls bouncing as she nodded. I turned to Ann. She looked stunning in her tunic. Her golden hoop earrings matched her eye shadow perfectly, the color complementing her honey eyes. She wore her shiny brown hair straight and parted to the side, bangs hanging just slightly below her eyebrows.

I looked at the three, marveling at their beauty and perfection. *I'm just as perfect, am I not? I am a Goddess as well.* I shoved down the rumblings in my head just in time to feel a question forming in Ann's.

"You have something to add, too?" I teased her.

"Yes!" she exploded, smiling. "Do you have the scroll with you?"

Before we'd parted at Gaianus, we'd made a promise to remain in contact by writing to each other on a scroll—the old-fashioned way. After one of us wrote something, that person would send it on to the next person. Chandra had started us out, and after I wrote, I was to give it to Ann.

"I'm sorry," I told her. "I don't have it." The three of them gasped and rolled their eyes. "I haven't had a chance to write."

"Oh really?" Chandra crossed her arms. "And can you explain why?"

I could feel her—more serious than teasing. Christy and Ann leaned in closer, intrigued.

"Well, I'm not going to Titanus." Chandra still had her arms crossed, so I continued, "I'm going to an all-mortal school in Colorado called Regis University."

I stopped to feel them. They were definitely confused.

"Wait, what?" they asked at the same time.

"Why?" Ann's face was incredulous.

"Well," I started to explain, but then the flashbacks started—coming home, seeing my father and then my brother, then my mother's long tale and her demand for my schooling. "It's a long story," was all I cared to say.

"That's weird," Christy said, "Regis University?" I felt her emotion shift from wonder to excitement. "That's the school my friend's boyfriend is going to!"

"Is your friend's boyfriend a God?" I asked.

She nodded and then sipped more wine from her chalice. "Yes, there are a few of them that go there."

"That's interesting," I muttered.

Suddenly, I felt him. I knew it was him because I felt a sense that only he had. I spotted him soon after, behind Christy, in a group of other Athletes. My breaths began to shorten.

"Brosi . . . Ambrosi?" one of my friends said. And then another,

"Petra?"

Finally, I felt Ann's worry. "What are you staring at?"

"More like who?" Christy added.

Chandra knew; I could feel it. I stared at her, almost as if asking permission. She nodded once.

I'm just going to talk to him. Just for a second.

"Excuse me real quick," I said, pushing past Christy and Ann—and their intrigued senses—and making my way through the drunken crowd of Deities.

This would be my only chance to talk to him, so I had to make the most of it. As I shoved my way through the last pack of huddled Deities, I saw a clear path to where he was standing. He looked beautiful—just as beautiful as when I had first seen him, and even more beautiful than when I had left him. He glowed in gold and yellow, his golden-brown hair spiked under his blue wreath, and he looked even more strapping as I moved closer. I felt the Gods surrounding him. The Athlete Gods were the easiest to sense—they reeked of pride and competition.

I reached his broad, sturdy back and hesitated to tap on it. When I finally summoned up the courage to do it and he turned around, he nearly missed me since he was so much taller. But then he tilted his head down, and I met his silver and blue eyes—the eyes that had first grabbed my attention, and the eyes that had dripped tears when I'd walked away. I could not feel pride now, only shock.

"Hey, Ricky," I managed to get out. Within seconds, I felt his passion sweep around us. It came through my fingers, up the sides of my arms and back, to the gentle part of my neck, and it crawled to my lips. It came so quickly I nearly fainted.

He turned around, gave a nod to the group of Athletes, and watched them walk away before turning back and meeting my eyes again. He stood like stone, and I felt the passion creep back down my lips, down my neck and back, down my arms, and off the tips of my fingers until it was gone and he was composed.

"Hey," he said lightly.

"How have you been?" I asked softly.

He bit his lip, and I involuntarily bit mine, too. His emotion was clear. I sensed it in him and through him, even as much as he tried to control it. "I shouldn't be here," I finally said.
"I'm sorry." I began to walk away but
he reached for me.

"No!"

I turned back, and his face fell—weak, broken again. His hand brushed the bottom of my cheek, and he tipped my head up to look at him. As my head lifted, I realized that his hand was not physically there. It had only been a sense. A sense I had felt so strongly, so tangibly from him.

"You don't have to go." His face was composed again. "How are you doing?"

I could still feel him fighting hard against his urge to caress my face, as well as Chandra's gaze behind me. I didn't need to look to know what she wanted—she was warning me. "*Make this conversation quick,*" I could almost hear her say. We could both feel his pain rising again.

"I'm okay," I answered.

"Where are you these days?" he asked, his voice calm.

I was a bit surprised at how well he was able to maintain his composure, but his words still carried his hurt to me.

I was already regretting having said hello.

"I'm at Regis University," I said quietly, and then, in response to his confusion, "In Colorado."

you?"

"A mortal school?" he asked, his eyes widening.

"Yes."

"Wow, you never cease to amaze me. Always full of surprises, aren't

I laughed at his ignorance. "Sure."

I felt someone staring at me—then two people. My exes, Silas and

Demyan. They were sidling up to the other blue-wreathed Athletes and to yet another ex-boyfriend of mine. Even though they stood quite a distance away from Ricky and me, I could feel their agitation. And I knew exactly why. They were talking about me, and they were mad—not at me, but at Ricky for talking to me.

"Well, I should really be going," I said quickly. "My parents are probably wondering where I am. It was good to see you again."

He hesitated, and I felt his anger rise. "Yeah, okay. Well, it was goo—"

I walked away before he could finish. I knew what he was going to say, and I had felt what he really meant. I glanced back just in time to see my other exes approaching Ricky.

It hadn't been the brightest move on my part; I had known his feelings for me would quickly grow beyond his control. Whether he knew it or not, the fact was simple: we could never be friends. Our friendship had been doomed from the instant we met. That was how it was . . . how it always ended with my relationships. I could never reciprocate the feelings he had for me. His memory held on to a fantasy of me, and he would continue to hold on to it until he created another one with someone else.

I ascended the stairway to the honorary seating section, where my family was located. Holding the green velvet curtain aside, I saw my father leaning on the gold railing with one hand. With his other hand, he held onto his cane. He looked so handsome in a white sarong with a green and gold twisted belt. My stunning mother stood on one side of him, wearing a white silk toga and green and gold ribbons in her hair. On the other side was only Eva, no John.

I came up behind them and wrapped my arms around my mother.

"Oh?" She turned, startled, and her eyes filled with tears when she saw me. "Petra!"

My father and Eva looked over, and their shouts echoed my mother's. Eva flew past our father, nearly tackling me with a big hug.

"When did you get here?" Father asked in his deep, smooth voice. He was the only one who was composed . . . as always.

"Only a few minutes ago. I stopped to talk to a couple friends before coming up."

"Did you see Chandra or Apria down there?" Eva asked. Her body was rigid, her emotions serious.

"Yes," I told her. "I saw them both. Why?"

She looked to my mother for comfort; the lounge was not large, so the tension quickly filled it.

"It doesn't matter what you are about to tell me. I won't care either way," I assured them. As the words left my mouth, the tension subsided as if someone had opened a window to release it.

"No one has seen or heard from John," Eva blurted.

Everyone waited and prepared themselves for my reaction. Still. After so many years of knowing me—and knowing that I was not capable of caring. Apria and Dion said I *should* care about things, but it all seemed very complicated.

"I'm sure he's fine. He probably needs some time alone still." The emotion finally subsided.

"Now, onto more intriguing news." I turned to my father. "Dad, why do you have a cane?"

His stone face melted, and he smiled. "My leg is acting up a bit." His voice was soft and reassuring—a good cover.

It was unsettling to see my father use a cane for support. He had fought in the Epigoni War and the Trojan War, battling alongside other legends like Achilles, Patroclus, Ajax, and Odysseus. My father was the legendary King of Argos, a God in Italy. After decades of ruling with great honor, he had been deemed worthy of immortality by Athena. And now he had fallen lame as the result of one cursed golden arrow. How unpredictable and fragile life was.

As I watched my father, I peered through the pinhole of mortality. I had never before known someone whose life had been so drastically and horrendously changed in one quick moment, by one accident. What a tragedy. Mortality was an odd thing to a God. How could it exist simultaneously with immortality? How did mortals never die out completely as a race when they could be killed so easily?

∞

The remaining days of the Ten-Day Celebration seemed to drag on, every day feeling the same. I couldn't remember what Via Olympia looked like without white robes and confetti everywhere. Some Gods never needed sleep, and some never got drunk, so the parties were endless. Plus, the Pentathlon had commenced, and after each win, there was a celebration. With the number of events and so many contestants winning, the celebrations quickly became redundant. And midnight tonight would be the most elaborate celebration of them all as we brought in the New Year.

After yet another Pentathlon event ended, I made my way up the stairs toward my family's lounge for some relaxation. I needed to put some distance between myself and Apria and Dion.

I didn't understand what they were holding back from me, but their resistance weighed on my body as if they were literally tugging at my skin.

Reaching the balcony room, I expected to see at least one of my family members, but it was empty. For a while I just reclined on one of the white klines and watched the different colored flower petals hover over the railing.

A golden bowl in the center of the table next to me was filled with my mother's dazzling red and pink peaches. I grabbed one and walked over to the railing, watching the huge crowds of lively, drunk Deities below. As I went to bite the peach, it slipped from my hand and fell. I didn't notice where it landed, for my eyes were glued to something I couldn't believe was real.

Athletes wearing white sarongs and blue wreaths were carrying a boy through the crowd of celebrating Deities, who cheered and threw palms and flowers at him. He must have been the final winner of the main event, for he sported a crown of olives over his blue wreath and a purple cloak over his sarong.

I was sure it was him. I remembered seeing his dimpled smile as he left Jaden's room one night. I leaned further over the railing, squinting to be sure. I could see his crystal blue eyes and deep dimples from where I stood. I had forgotten his name, but I remembered he was an athlete at Regis—a basketball player.

My eyes remained glued as I watched him being paraded through the crowd. Curiosity finally getting the better of me, I made a dash toward the stairs. My plan was to talk to him and confirm that he was the boy I'd seen at Regis. And if he was, I had so much to ask him. For one, why was he attending a mortal school? He looked too young.

I jumped down the last four stairs, turned into the street, and was quickly blocked by the wall of togas crowding around the boys who carried him. There was no way my plan was going to work. Too many Deities surrounded him.

I was turning to head back to the lounge when I noticed another familiar face. She stood with two other Deities who laughed at the overexcited crowd. Her hands rested in her handmade sarong pockets. The silver wreath she wore was tilted, and she smiled smugly. She was a small Goddess, and had the most unbelievable mahogany skin, gleaming with an airbrushed glow. She looked fragile, but exuded confidence and wisdom. Her friends wore identical togas with handmade pockets, but their wreaths were purple like Dion's.

Something struck me as odd about the way they kept their hands in their pockets, but I stopped staring and continued toward the stairway. As I lifted my foot to the first stair, I felt something peculiar but exciting. Trying to track where the sense was coming from, I zeroed in on the trio of Deities, and looking right back at me was the Goddess I had noticed first. She tilted her head, looking peculiarly at me.

Our eyes met, and she smiled. A drifting rose petal fell onto her shoulder. She watched to see if it would fall off, but it remained, so she lifted her hand from her pocket and brushed the petal off. In that brief wave of her hand, I saw a brand identical to Dion's on the inside of her wrist. My mouth fell open. She looked at me, narrowing her eyes, not angrily, but thoughtfully.

71

Trying to act as if I hadn't seen anything, I quickly turned around and headed up the stairs.

With each step, I thought back to what I'd just seen. Now the handmade pockets made sense. Were they all Lambdas? I was surprised they hadn't been kicked out of the Heavens yet. For that matter, I was surprised Dion hadn't been kicked out. I cringed at the horrible thought. He could be sent to Tartarus if he wasn't careful to keep the brand hidden.

I reached the balcony and assumed my previous position—leaning on the railing, surveying the crowd of togas once again. I stayed there until the orange sunset disappeared over the marble buildings across from me. The sky bled out its last colors, and then night moved in with its silver stars. The celebrations from below grew louder than ever. More flower petals and confetti fell, followed by animated fireworks. I looked back at the empty lounge. I was bringing in the New Year alone. And then an unexpected thought crept into my mind.

I was ready to go back to Earth.

Chapter 14

Game Night

Dear Ann,

I apologize for the delay. I was able to find the scroll hidden in the corner of my closet. Please excuse the crease—one of my books landed on it. Anyway, so I am sitting—well lying—in my bed, and it's three in the morning. I really don't know why I'm not able to sleep at night anymore—a lot on my mind, I suppose. Most of the time, I think of what it is I might not find. I don't know if I would see anything even if it were staring me in the face.
I know you thought you would never hear me say this, but . . . I hate not being able to feel. I don't know how this could ever be considered a gift. If I'd had the ability to choose my gift, I would never have chosen this one. It's lonely, though I know it did not seem that way at Gaianus. I honestly don't know how you ladies even put up with me. Tolerance is your gift. You love me for me.
But will I ever love? Will I ever meet a God who could make me feel that emotion? And when I do meet him, will I be ready? I can only ask for the sun to warm my heart and for Helios 'chariot to ride over my eyes to see the light . . .
I hope you are well. I miss you all.
Truly
your's
petra

∞

"Have you talked to Britta since you've been back?" Jaden asked, her green eyes wide with curiosity.

"Yes," I told her, my voice muffled as I put on my sweatshirt, struggling to find the opening. I finally popped my head through to see her looking at me, dumbfounded.

"Did she apologize?" she asked, sounding annoyed. She had been leaning against the doorway but now came in and plopped herself on my bed.

"Not exactly," I said as I put on my shoes. "Did she tell you about game night tonight?"

"No!" Jaden's face scrunched up as if she had just caught a whiff of something unpleasant.

"I guess she invited Taylor and Tawny over, too."

"Oh," she sulked. "Well, I'm going out anyway. Have fun with her, though," she added sarcastically over her shoulder as she left the room. I laughed.

The doorbell rang. Britta yelled that she would get it. Entering the living room, I saw the game already laid out, ready to be played.

"*Brosi!*" Tawny and Montana sauntered around the corner from the hallway and into the living room. Britta followed behind them, a serious sense trailing her.

I greeted Tawny with a hug but stopped when I saw Montana. She looked different somehow, leaner than before—every bit of muscle on her was toned, chiseled as if she were a wooden carving. She was much tanner, too, looking as if she had spent her entire break on a tropical island. Her brown hair no longer had blonde highlights but was a solid gold shade. And although she wore it up in a ponytail, I could see it had also grown in length. When I hugged her, she felt like cold, soft granite. She reminded me of the Athlete Goddesses.

"How are you guys?" I asked.

"How was your winter break?" Britta asked at the same time.

"Good," Tawny replied cheerfully. "Hung out with the family."

I looked at Montana, but all she did was smile and nod her head, then redirect the question to me. "How was yours?"

"Mine was nice." I tried to smile pleasantly back at the glare in her eyes.

"Alright, guys, let's partner up," Britta demanded. "Tawny and I will be on one team, and Taylor and Petra on the other."

Tawny rolled the dice and then moved their piece, counting each space before planting it in the final spot. Then she reached over and pulled a card from the deck. Her eyes pinched as she read it and she let out a loud laugh.

The card told us we were supposed to act out a movie—similar to charades—and Montana and Britta were supposed to guess what it was. Tawny and I started pantomiming what was explained on the card. She motioned me to get down on my knees, and then she stood up behind me, holding my arms out to the side as if I was flying.

"Shipwreck!" Britta and Montana yelled at the same time.

"Yeah!" we shouted back at them.

"Taylor, your guess was a little behind," Tawny teased.

"No way," she argued.

"Okay, whatever. We both get points," Britta determined.

I high-fived Montana and then plopped myself on the couch next to her. As I sat down, my hand gently brushed against hers. Her body stiffened immediately, and my mind stopped. Suddenly, it was as though the room filled with water. The inside of my body shrunk and then expanded slowly. Voices slowed down, and movements became still. I felt every vein in her body become engorged with blood. I felt her heartbeat in my eardrums, in my chest,

74

in my veins—pounding faster and faster, tensing my every muscle. I held my body rigid to avoid any sudden movement that might disrupt the moment, fascinated by how her body had reacted to my touch and that I was able to feel something from her.

"Hey, guys!" I heard a voice say.

And with that, Montana's pounding heart quieted, her body loosened, my body returned to normal, and the water was flushed from the room.

The four of us looked up to see Jaden and Diane with four guys. Three I recognized from their frequent evening visits, but this was the first time I had seen them all together. They had graduated from Regis just this past year. Each wore a tight white T-shirt that emphasized bulging muscles. Three of the four were nearly giants, while the fourth guy was significantly shorter. I had never seen him before—most likely a new victim—and he definitely stood out. He was incredibly good-looking—even more so when he smiled. His dark waves curled in no particular direction, wrapping up and around the edge of his charcoal fedora. He wore an unbuttoned black vest atop a V-neck T-shirt, and diamond earrings.

Before I could stop myself, my attention was focused on him, a panther sizing up her prey. Jaden was introducing them to us, but I wasn't really listening until she spoke my name. As she did, his eyes finally met mine, and he smiled. He had the greenest eyes I had ever seen, and they shone as they peeked at me through the shadow of his fedora. He was adorable—and breathtaking. I could have him by the end of the night.

Old habits die hard.

"We're just getting back from the club," Diane said.

I looked at the clock—it was already midnight.

"Yeah, it was lame," the bulkiest one of the foursome added with a crooked grin.

I shook my head, trying to shake the thoughts out. I didn't want to revert to how I used to be. I wanted a fresh start—one where I didn't hurt anyone and could hopefully learn how to feel.

Montana was eyeing the same guy I was. I felt her warm breath as she gasped in and out, as if he had taken her breath away. *Good.* I needed someone else to be interested in him so I would have to stay away.

If I really wanted a God, I would go for it. But if another Goddess—or in this case, mortal girl—wanted the same God or mortal guy that I had eyes for, I would always move on to the next victim. There was too much to deal with when in competition for the same guy. Plus, I didn't want to stand in the way of someone who might actually feel something real.

I directed all of my attention back to the board game—focusing there until the conversations ended and the guys finally moved down the hallway with Diane and Jaden.

As we returned to the game, I felt Montana's body tense, but I couldn't sense anything more of her feelings. When the game finally ended, Britta and

Tawny stood up, flailing their arms in the air, screaming in celebration of their victory.

Tawny received a phone call and headed outside to answer, and Britta began putting the board game away while Montana and I sat on the couch talking about what she had done over winter break. My cheeks started to ache from laughing so hard at all of the funny stories she told.

Britta's voice soon traveled to the living room from the kitchen, where she was talking loudly on the phone as she put away dishes. Instinctively, I felt it coming. Her voice rose from a soft but firm tone to a threatening screech. It was obviously Alan on the receiving end.

Montana and I kept talking, trying to ignore her cursing.

Her eyes soon flicked to something above and behind me, following the moving object until her eyes focused to the left of me.

"Is this your house, too?" I heard a low, sexy voice intone, enunciating each word slowly and delicately. I tilted my head back and saw the crystal green eyes under the fedora.

The room filled with tension, and I breathed in an intoxicating mix of adrenaline and anxiety. I sat there absorbing what I was sensing from him. "Yes," I finally blurted.

"Well, it's quite a beautiful house." He smiled and stretched his hand toward me. I reached for it, sliding my palm into his to shake. His body remained calm, but I sensed his silent inquiry. His hand was strong but soft— warm like Hades 'fire.

"I'm Nick Herms," he said, grinning. "But everyone calls me Herms."

Herms! Of course! His name was the key to the mystery. The Messenger God, Hermes himself.

I glanced at Montana. She was focused on him, and her face showed pain. Was his beauty too overwhelming for her? She looked devastated, but I could not feel why.

"I'm Petra Ambrosi," I said brusquely. "And this is Taylor Letto."

His eyes blinked when he heard her name, and Montana grinned. For just a moment, I sensed an acknowledgment within him. Something heavy.

He knew something I did not. I looked back at Montana, feeling them as they shook hands. The aura in the room had flipped from excitement to an unexpected steadiness.

"Well," I spoke up, yawning, "I should be going to bed."

"I should, too," Montana added. "I need to find Tawny, though. She has my keys."

I thanked Montana for coming, nodded courteously at Nick, and headed down the hallway to my bedroom. Quickly, I changed into my pajamas and dove into bed before the cold had a chance to sneak in. Shutting my eyes, I tried to convince myself it would be easy to fall asleep tonight, but I ended up awake as usual, staring at my closed eyelids. I reached for my radio and turned it on. A melancholy piano tune poured from the speakers, and I cuddled up and shut my eyes again for a second attempt.

There was a soft knock at the door. I opened my eyes. When I didn't hear it a second time, I closed my eyes again, thinking the knocker had gone away. But then I heard it again, just as soft as the first time.

"Yes?" I whispered. I figured I didn't need to get up to answer it.

"May I come in?" a voice asked.

"Yes?"

The door opened.

"Were you sleeping?" the silhouette asked.

"I was trying." I still couldn't see who it was. The shadow moved closer, into the bluish-grey light coming through my window. Nick. I barely recognized him without his fedora, and his green eyes now looked dark.

"I'm sorry," he said, sounding sincere. "I was wondering . . ." he paused, trying to fit his words together just right. "My ride seems to be occupied, and it looks like I won't be leaving any time soon. May I stay and chat with you?"

I didn't know whether this was an extremely polite way of asking if he could attempt to make out with me, or if he was actually being genuine.

However, I did not sense any ulterior motive.

"Sure."

He took his shoes off and settled himself easily next to me. Gently placing his head on the pillow next to mine, he studied the dark ceiling above; I followed his lead.

I began to search for any emotions he unconsciously leaked, but I could find none—his emotions were as empty as the ceiling. I wished for sleep to overcome me. It was both strange and perplexing to know that I could be with a God—a very attractive God—and not want to do anything but sleep.

He was lying in my bed, helpless, and I had absolutely no desire to take him.

My neck involuntarily started to turn to look at him. He was incredibly beautiful in the grey light—it lit up his eyes and cast a mysterious shadow over his olive skin. He shifted back to stare at the ceiling but scooted closer to me as he did so. His head brushed my temple. His body was incredibly warm; I could feel the heat emanating from it.

"So where are *you* from?" he finally asked, breaking the silence. My mind started whirling. I didn't know what to tell him, so I went with my default reply. "Texas . . ."

Even in the semi-darkness, I could feel his smile. He seemed amused by my answer. "Oh yeah?" he asked teasingly. "What part?"

I was stumped. I had no idea what part. No one had ever probed past Texas. I ducked my head into my blanket, thinking maybe if I pretended to be asleep, he would go away. I would rather not answer than tell a lie.

I felt his anticipation, waiting for my answer. After a few minutes, he reached over me, and his warm fingertips gently caressed my neck and chin. He grasped my chin and turned me to face him, until I gazed upon his perfectly proportioned lips.

"That's not where you're from, Petra," he said softly.

What would normally annoy me was said too sensually to argue with—and Nick was much too cute to assault. He smiled at me, charmingly, convincingly, and then brought his face closer to mine. Mere centimeters away, he stopped. I could sense his thrill, could hear the beating of his heart, feel it vibrating through the sheets. I closed the distance and fit my lips to his, delicately kissing him. His hand clutched the back of my neck, and I buried my hands in his unruly black curls. I felt his body warming, felt his pounding heart. It got harder and harder, louder and louder, sounding like a knock at the door.

Knock, knock, knock. So gentle and soft, but clear enough to be heard. I pulled back. There were three more knocks on the bedroom door. This time, both of us heard them.

"Brosi? You awake?" a voice whispered from the other side of the door.

Without hesitation, I bounded over Nick and stumbled my way to the door. I swung it open to catch Montana with her arm raised, prepared to knock again. She saw Nick lying in my bed, and then looked back to me.

"Looks like you *are* awake," she said.

I shook my head and laughed. "Uh, what's up?"

"I can't find Tawny, and Sade isn't answering her phone. Can I stay the night here?" Her cheeks were flushed a bit—I'd never seen Montana blush before.

"Of course," I said without hesitation.

"Thank you." She looked at Nick again. "I'll be out in the living room."

I chuckled at her valiant attempt to give me privacy, but the thought of making her sleep in the living room alone did not sit well with me. Plus, if she stayed here in the room, it would prevent anything more from happening with Nick. So, I gave her some extra pajamas and jumped back into bed next to Nick, beckoning Montana to join us on my other side.

We stayed up talking about school and about things both relevant and irrelevant for quite some time before my eyelids started getting heavy. I tried to stay awake, but my eyes kept closing involuntarily. Every now and then, I heard snippets of Montana and Nick's continuing dialogue. Eventually, I allowed myself to fall asleep.

When I awoke, they were asleep. Both slept on their sides, facing me. It was even warmer now that I had two bodies so close to me. I closed my eyes again, trying to fall back asleep, but soon felt a tug on my left elbow. Montana tugged me once more, grabbing my sweatshirt and pulling me closer.

Assuming she was cold, I scooted a bit closer to her. She reached for my arm and wrapped herself up in it, like a child cuddling with a teddy bear. I was confused and unsure what to do. No one had ever done anything like that, and I had never let anyone touch me as she was.

The bed shook suddenly as Nick rolled to his side and wrapped his legs into mine as a snake would wrap around its prey.

I was wide awake now. There was no way I could sleep with the both of them wrapped around me like this.

I felt suffocated, but my body reacted—typically—without feeling. Eyes open, limbs stiff, and thoughts blank.

Montana's face was buried in my arm. Every couple of seconds, I would get a tug from her. I didn't know what she wanted, and I could not sense a thing she was feeling. Only her heartbeat was my lead—it rose with excitement and then slowed as she tucked even deeper into my arm.

I didn't quite understand what was happening, but I wanted it to end. I just wanted to sleep. I unraveled my arm from Montana and my leg from Nick, deciding that maybe I would have a better outcome sleeping on my stomach, but just as I had gotten into a comfortable position, their limbs wrapped around me again—Nick around my leg and Montana around my arms. It was like dueling bodies.

This time I sensed weakness from one of them. *Montana?* I felt myself torn between the two—the gorgeous, green-eyed Nick and the vulnerable Montana. My body yearned for Montana, and I had no idea what it was that lured me.

Nick's body wanted more than cuddling. He wanted my lips—and more. I could sense that, almost too easily. I thought about kissing him, resuming where we had left off, but I shook my head to clear that thought from my mind, moving closer to Montana. I relinquished and allowed her to tuck her body into me and wrap her arms around mine. I felt her relax, which allowed my stiff body to soften as well. I felt her soft breathing and matched it with my own. Her heartbeat grew softer and her breath fainter until I felt her fall soundly asleep, completely unaware of the momentous thing that had just happened.

Chapter 15

Nick Herms

Montana and Nick were both gone when I awoke the next morning. When I saw Montana later that day, she was timid at first. I didn't sense it from her, but saw it in her body language. She wouldn't even look me in the eye. Her discomfort was mystifying; she was definitely not her normal self as she told me she was leaving with a friend for the weekend. Throughout the brief conversation, I felt as if she needed something. She was quick and inexpressive but then lingered afterward, as if she thought I was going to say something. I left her with a big smile and a goodbye hug—and that was that. My smile was my shield. I had learned that it was what made people happy. I could sense it from them—the happiness that oozed from their insides. It was amazing that a simple action like that—something any mortal or immortal could easily do—could make a being feel so warm and cozy inside, even if only for a brief second. So I smiled a *lot*.

The rest of the day dragged by. I had nothing to do. Well, actually, I did have a stack of books I needed to read, but I was only two sentences into one when I was interrupted by a knock on the front door. I dropped my book to the floor to see who it was.

He stood with his head tilted slightly downward, his eyes glimmering from below a black fedora this time. His hands were hidden behind his back. I lowered my eyes to his feet and saw they were bare.

"Nick, why are you barefoot? Did you lose your winged sandals?" I teased.

He let out a great guffaw and then showed himself into my house, the room filling with his ego.

"Petra," he said, still laughing, "it's good to see you again, too."

"What's up?"

He apparently thought that a crass response because he gave me a look of disdain before relaxing and giving me an easy smile. "We didn't get to talk much last night, so I thought we could do that today."

His brashness got the best of him, and he moved into the kitchen, helping himself to the food in our fridge. I noticed that he still held his right arm against the other side of his body, keeping his hand from my view.

"What else do we have to talk about?"

"A lot!" he said patronizingly.

I eyed him, watching him select the second half of a sandwich I had planned to have for dinner. He bit into it like a starved beast that had not eaten in years. Even with the disgusting and unmannerly way he was eating, I still found him beautiful to watch. He swallowed another bite before continuing.

"Petra, do you know who I am?" His voice was quiet, but deep, and his accent easily flowed this time, for he did not hold it back. For a moment, I thought I was back in the Heavens, trying to glean meaning from the Elders ' thickly accented words.

I hesitated for the longest time. Was it a trick question? The sense flowing through him was as calm as my steady heartbeat. I went with the most obvious answer.

"You're Nick."

He ceased his chewing as he waited for me to continue. The feeling in his chest intensified with every click of the second hand on the clock. "Descendant of Hermes . . . the Messenger God." There was no question in my voice, and no disagreement in his grin. "I was serious about your sandals."

He suddenly revealed his hidden hand, extended his arm, and dropped the winged sandals onto the counter, smiling mischievously. In a blink, he was in front of me, inches from my face, each breath tickling my nose. In his breath, I could sense it all. I felt something threatening and knew that what he was about to say was serious. I sucked in his breath, feeling him, and waited.

"I'm here to give you a message from the Horai." His teeth clenched as he spoke, his tone ominous.

"The Horai?" I asked. My lips felt dry. The Horai were the three sister Goddesses who guarded the gates of Olympus. The Elders 'superiors. No one ever dealt with them personally. We called them the Hours—Justice, Law, and Peace, wearing masks of beauty. To receive a message from them meant something extraordinary had happened: the Moirai, the three Agents of Destiny, had seen something in your destiny.
A large lump formed in the back of my throat, and I tried swallowing it down, gulping loudly.

"What's the message?" I asked. I thought seriously about grabbing his lips with mine, but he moved back before I could decide. His lips puckered with every breath I released from my lips.

His emotions wavered—to kiss or not to kiss? And then he opened his mouth to speak. "They said to be careful with your actions."
I found myself more focused on his mouth and lips than on the threat he had delivered—the threat from the Horai.
He moved still closer, touching his cheek to mine, and whispered into my ear, "They will be watching you." The threat sounded so soft and beautiful, but the feeling behind it was anything but.

He rubbed his cheek against mine as he backed away and stood to face me. Before he could pull away further, I brushed my lips against his, only for a second. That was all I needed. I felt him melt, and the ego that had once filled the room quickly dissolved. I walked to the front door, waiting for him to follow me.

He was soon trailing behind me in a drunken trance. He had gotten too close for his own good. The tease had a pull on him, making it hard for him to control what he was feeling. I looked into his face and felt his wish for composure.

81

I stood at the door, waiting for his idle pace to quicken. As he reached the door, he turned back to gaze upon me. His mouth hung open in awe, his eyes were glazed over, and his mind was lost in flights of fancy. I had seen an identical look on other Gods 'faces too many times before. Seducing him had been a mistake.

"Thank you for coming, Nick," I said, speaking to the ground.

He nodded and walked out. Quickly, I closed the door behind him and went straight to my bedroom, collapsing on my bed. My mind immediately began to work, and I squeezed my pillow until the feathers burst from the seams.

I didn't understand Nick's message. The Horai would be watching my actions? Was I supposed to do nothing until someone told me it was safe? I grabbed my other pillow and dove into it, squeezing my eyes shut and praying for sleep to take me. There the Horai could not watch me. There my actions could not be condemned.

Chapter 16

Lighting the Charge

When I woke up on Sunday, it felt as if I had been asleep the whole time Montana was gone, only to be awakened by her text.

"Hey, are you busy tonight?"

"No, just homework and
trying to sleep." "I need to
talk to you."

"Okay, when?"

"Half hour? Can you meet me at my
place?" "Okay, sounds good."

When I stepped outside, it was a lot colder than I'd anticipated. Snow had fallen, covering everything in sight—roofs, lawns, and streets. I went back in and headed down the hallway to Jaden's room. Her door was open, and her bedroom light shined into the dark hallway. She sat cross-legged, holding an oversized textbook. I stepped into the triangle of light and leaned on her doorway.

She smiled instantly when she saw me, letting off warming waves. "Hey! What's up?"

"Can I ask you for a favor?"

Her smile turned into a laugh. "Of course," she said without hesitation.

"May I borrow your truck for a couple hours? I—"

"Go right ahead," she said quickly, cutting me off. "The keys are on the kitchen counter."

One thing I enjoyed about Jaden was that her aura always felt light and warm—loving. I never felt anything negative from her. She had a good heart. What I also liked about her was that she never asked too many questions, so I never had to tell her a lie.

"Thank you." I gave her a final smile before turning to leave, but then stopped and turned back to her. "I'll be quick. I just have to talk to Taylor for a bit." I didn't know why, but I wanted to let her know where I was going.

She smiled and nodded. "Sounds good!"

There was an eerie feeling in the air. It must have been the fog, which made it a lot harder to see. Montana was not hard to find, though; she sat on the curb outside her townhouse. She wore her hair down—it was a lot longer than I expected, spilling out from one side of the hood that covered her eyes—and didn't look like herself.

I drove up to the curb cautiously, wiping condensation from the windshield. She popped up and quickly jumped into the truck.

"Hey," she said, rubbing her hands together. "It's so warm in here." She reached forward and covered the vents with her hands. "Is this new?"

"It's Jaden's. I won't have my truck back until the end of summer." She seemed immersed in her own thoughts as she continued rubbing her hands together near the vents.

"So how was your trip?" I asked, trying to pull her into a conversation. Her expression told me she had no idea what I was talking about, but then she seemed to suddenly remember.

"It was good," she answered curtly, plainly, with no elaboration. I expected nothing more than that from her. "You want to maybe . . . go somewhere?"

"Sure, where?"

"The baseball stadium?"

"Okay," I said.

But I must have hesitated, because she said, "We don't have to. If you don't—"

"Baseball stadium sounds fun," I said. "It's adventurous." I gave her a smile.

We hopped the stadium's fence and made our way toward the announcer's booth. Surprisingly, the door was unlocked. We entered the booth and found two folding chairs inside.

"So, what's up?" I asked, sitting down in one of the chairs. I wanted her to say what she wanted to say quickly, before it was too cold for either of us to say anything.

"Nothing," she said. "I just needed to get out of my dorm." She grew rigid in her seat, and she wrapped her arms around herself as if her stomach ached.

"Are you still cold?" I asked.

"No, I'm fine." She pulled her hood off, unveiling her long, golden blonde hair.

My eyes became fixated on that hair for a moment, but I shook it off and continued to question her. "What is it, Taylor?"

The heat from my breath collaborated with the cold, dancing and swirling into clouds.

"Petra," she said softly, "I sort of . . . want to tell you something." Her voice sounded as sensual as Nick's had the night he slept over. She had captured my attention. I leaned in closer and nodded for her to continue. *Should I be worried or scared or happy?* Had she finally discovered I was not like her? That I was a different being from a different place? If so, how would I react?

She leaned in, too, and I waited. The temperature seemed to be dropping every second. I watched as her face morphed with each different expression. She bit her lip as if nervous, pinched her eyebrows in concentration, and then lifted them back up, which made me think she was ready to speak. She drew in a deep breath, and then let it out gently. I watched her warm breath curl in front of her lips. She leaned in even closer, shivering, and she stared at the floor.

84

I decided to lean in with her, giving her the heat from my body.

Every breath she let out formed a cloud, inches from my nose. Those puffs of air spoke more to me than her words.

Maybe I should try to help her explain? "Are you hurt?" I asked softly, thinking I would go with yes-or-no questions to start, even if they seemed ridiculous.

"No," she said, sighing out another breath.

"Is everything okay?"

She raised her head slightly, but then let it fall back down. "No," she admitted.

Whatever she needed to say was tearing her up inside. "Are you confused about something?"

Her head lifted, and in the moon's light, I saw her eyes widen. She did not answer, but her expression spoke for her. Her eyebrows lifted with worry, and her teeth fastened on her bottom lip again. She stared at me like that for a while and then nodded her head.

"About?" I probed. But she sat still and silent, hoping I would finish the thought for her. "Are you wanting to switch majors?"

She shook her head.

"Religion?" I asked gently. She gave me a confused look, and then shook her head. "Political party?" I tried to make her smile, but she just looked frustrated. I laughed, which made her ease up slightly and giggle a bit. She reached for my hand and slid her chilled fingers between mine. Although our hands were icy cold, I was warmed instantly by her touch, and one more question came to mind.

"Your sexual orientation?" I asked softly.

She started to lift her head but stopped. Quickly, she looked down again, opening her mouth like she was ready to talk. I held my breath as I waited for her response. Had I been too bold? I wanted her to know that it did not matter to me if she liked girls.

I began to think about Dion and the Lambda—the brand of the Enlightened. During the Ten-Day Celebration, Dion had talked drunkenly about the God he had fallen in love with and exactly how he had received his Lambda brand. He was a mess—slurring his words, making no sense whatsoever, and crying as he told me he had to say goodbye to this God in order to remain in the Heavens before his trial with the Moirai.

The Lambdas were called The Enlightened because of their wholeness in accepting love with all genders. Dion said that in love, gender did not matter—it was about the connecting of souls. He'd explained it as being like negative and positive charges. If a person had a negative charge, that person would eventually find their positive. It didn't matter which gender held the opposing charge; one would be powerfully drawn to the other. Dion told me that we should not be the ones to judge and choose who we are drawn to, for if we limit ourselves, we may never find Fate's match for us, nor will we ever know ourselves.

The body—the carrier—of the one holding your opposite charge was irrelevant. The Enlightened looked past the physical body to the intense passion in that charge.

Montana's nerves did not show any sign of dwindling. The dim moonlight streaming into the booth embraced her blushing cheeks. I kept my eyes riveted to her, and she focused hers on the floor. Even without my gift, I would have been able to sense her embarrassment.

" I don't care," I told her as convincingly as I could. I scooted in closer in an attempt to calm her nerves.

Finally, she looked up from the floor—not at me, but past my shoulder, behind me. "That's not it," she whispered and grabbed my other hand. She was as cold as ice and began to shiver.

"Tay, you're freezing," I said, bringing her hands together between mine and rubbing them to warm them. When that didn't seem to work, I moved them close to my mouth and started to blow my hot breath on them. She nervously tried to pull her hands from mine as if I had cut her. I let go immediately, but her hands lingered near my lips.

Suddenly, her fingertips gently brushed against my cheeks and then my lips. I had no idea what expression showed on my face. It must have mirrored hers as she became conscious of what she was doing. I didn't move, not wanting to be rude. *She meant no harm,* I told myself. My mouth opened, breathing in deeper than I needed to. Clouds of breath formed between us— touching, kissing. We remained still, not looking at one another.

"Taylor," I said, breaking the frozen silence. Her eyes peeked up from underneath her eyebrows. I took one long breath. "I'm here." My voice came out raspy. "If you ever need anything, I'm here for you."

She sat up, adjusting herself in the seat. Then she stood, gave me a small nod, and walked out.

Chapter 17

The Enlightenment

I sat scrunched up on my bed doing homework, but the noise of the various emotions I sensed outside my door made it hard. Lately, I hadn't been able to concentrate well. All my time was spent with Montana. After our talk, things had changed.

Suddenly, I sensed his ego coming down the hallway toward my room. Lifting my eyes from my book, I stared at my bedroom door. It swung open, and Nick entered.

"Hey, Nick."

"Hey, beautiful. What're you doing?" He stepped in and plopped down on my bed.

"Homework. What are you doing here?"

"I'm here to see you, of course," he said with a charming grin. I could feel he wanted something. "How long are you going to be with that?"

My eyes narrowed as I finished sensing what he wanted. "Why?" I asked, my voice low.

His head tilted, and he smiled again. In that instant, my sense of him was so detailed and precise that I could almost see the picture he was drawing in his head.

"Are you horny?" I asked, amused.

His smile fell, and the somewhat obscene thought bubble in his mind burst.

"H–How did . . .? . . . That's your gift, isn't it?" He reared back as if frightened. "You can read people's thoughts?"

"No!" I laughed. "No, I cannot read thoughts." I set down my book and sat up in my bed. "I can feel your emotions—which are very strong right now, by the way."

"W–Well, I'm sorry. You just act like . . ." He lowered his gaze.

"Like what?" I asked.

head. "Like you know what you're doing," he said, chuckling and shaking his

I knew what he was implying. He thought I was a *poutana*—a tramp.

It was the implication every God made after been bitten by my seduction.

"I'm sorry," he said, shaking his head as if shaking off the seduction. "I'm sorry I thought that about you." He hesitated. "Do you do it . . . ever?"
I shook my head slowly.

"Wow. Why not?"

I shrugged. "I'm waiting, I suppose."

"For what?" he asked critically. "Me?" He grinned.

"No," I said. "Love."

"Well, good luck with that!" He bit his bottom lip, trying to hold his tongue. But in the end, he spoke anyway. "Wow, I can't believe virgins still exist. And I would have never thought you were one. You don't act like one at all."
I nodded in automatic response. These were words I had heard many times before. Same process, same routine. The final stage of seduction: the hard truth.

"I mean, Petra . . . Don't tell me you don't know you are sexy, because you are . . ." He licked his top lip. "*Very* sexy."

He reeked of what he craved. It was all disgustingly familiar. Words I had heard repeatedly—all leading to broken hearts. I had done exactly what I had promised not to do when I first came to Regis. It was as if I had become the victim of my own powerful game. I persuaded males—Gods or mortals— to play by simply knowing what they felt and then acting accordingly, provoking them and making them feel like they desired me. It was called a *gift* to be the Goddess of Emotion. But it was a curse.

"Okay, Nick." I patted him on the shoulder and stood. Without missing a beat, I grabbed my jacket, left the room, and hurried down the hall and out the front door.

∞

Not really knowing where I was going, I found myself at Sunflower Market. I headed straight to the wine section—Nouveau, Lambrusco, Sangria, it didn't matter. Anything to help me stop my spinning thoughts and fall asleep.

"Petra?"

I turned toward the soft voice. Montana stood there, holding a bottle of Merlot.

"Hey," I said, eyeing her and then the bottle. She looked at the bottle and then back at me, smiling guiltily. "Sade and Tawny went out. I decided to enjoy the night to myself."

I nodded, and a long silence followed.

"What are you up to tonight?" she finally asked.

"Jaden and Diane have people over," I said. "I just needed to get out."

Every day was a party at our house. Jaden and Diane had an open-door policy when it came to guys. I never did ask if they really were nymphets. Jessica and I had given them that label as a joke, but since I'd been living with them, it was starting to seem more and more like a real possibility.

"How are you supposed to buy that?" Montana asked, eyeing my Lambrusco.

"Oh." I had forgotten. "You're right." I was only twenty on Earth, not legally of age to buy alcohol in North America.

I started to put the bottle back, but Montana walked over and grabbed it out of my hand. "I got you."

"No!" But before I could fight her on it, she was already heading to the cashier. I chased her down the aisle, trying to grab her from behind. She swung her arm behind her, swiping at my hands. When she reached the cashier, she had already pulled out her money, so I gave up the fight.

"So what are you doing for the rest of the night?" she asked as she grabbed the receipt.

"I don't know," I said, pondering what I should do. "I just don't want to go back home."

"Cool," she said abruptly. "Come over, and we'll watch a movie." I met her eyes and found myself nodding my head.

When we entered her townhouse, I jumped into my usual spot on the couch and put the two bottles on the wooden table. Montana brought two glasses from the kitchen, set them down, and handed me the opener. As I opened the bottles, she popped in a movie.

"What are we watching?"

"Shipwreck

" "Yay." I teased She gave me a sour look as she sat on the other couch, but grinned when she said, "I knew you would be excited."

We ended up talking through most of the movie.

"What's your favorite song right now?" she asked while pouring more wine.

I chugged what was left in my glass before answering. "I would still have to say the same song. 'The Nicest Thing 'by Kate Nash." She tilted her head and took a sip from her glass.

"It's a good song," I continued. "It's all about love—what you can ask from love."

She began to giggle behind her glass. "You can't ask love anything."

I squinted at her, questioning what she meant by that. I wished I could feel what she meant, wished I could sense her.

"I can ask why you're sitting so far away," I stated bluntly but teasingly. "Come here."

She looked at me for what seemed like a very long time before hesitantly getting up. She picked up the bottle, handing it to me as she sat down.

"You have to finish it. I'm done."

I took the bottle from her, leaned back into the couch, and gulped down the rest. After placing the empty bottle on the table, I rested my head on the back of the sofa.

"What did you mean when you said you can't ask love anything?" I asked, staring at the blank ceiling. My eyes were heavy, drooping more every second until they finally fell shut.

I felt my nose itching as if a feather was tickling it and opened my eyes to find Montana standing over me, grinning. It was the tips of her hair that had been tickling my nose.

"Because it's not anyone's right to ask love anything," she said as she leaned closer, reaching for my shoulders to help me sit up. "Love has its own agenda."

How strange that she spoke of love as if it were a person. I chuckled to myself, wondering what she would do if she knew my brother was the God of Love.

She reached out her hand to help me up from the sofa. I stood quickly and became dizzy, leaning on her like a crutch. She hobbled with me to her bed, where I curled up in the corner against the wall.

"I'm tired," I managed to mutter.

She hopped in after me and turned off the light. "I know you're tired—that's why I brought you to bed."

I rolled myself over to face her and gave her a loose, one-armed hug.

"Thanks for caring," I mumbled and collapsed into a deep sleep.

∞

I wasn't sure how long I slept, but when I woke up, Montana was asleep, her face only inches from mine. I realized I was lying slightly on her side of the bed, so I rolled onto my back and scooted closer to the wall. As I did, she gently grabbed my shirt and tugged me back toward her. I shifted back to my original position, and her leg moved from beneath the sheets to slip perfectly between mine. She scooted closer, until our lips were close enough to touch.

I stiffened and held my breath, not wanting to move any part of my body. Her breath pulled at my lips, and her nose skimmed the tip of mine.

91

I was stone—I couldn't have moved even if I'd tried. Or was it that I just didn't want to? Her leg was soft and warm between mine—something I had never before experienced. Her foot coiled around mine. My eyes widened and I gasped.

As we lay there, our bodies entwined like a twisted braid, I couldn't ignore it anymore. I felt it over me, around me—a layer of warmth surrounding us. The feeling was very much alive, creeping in and out of every pore of my body. I yearned for the lips that I knew wanted mine, and I didn't need to lean in too far for them to meet. Tentatively. Delicately.

I had just unleashed something—a beautiful beast birthed within the both of us. I slipped away, back onto my pillow, still entwined with the body that warmed me.

After our lips 'greeting, the reveling began—and then a cloud of fear right after. I realized it was emanating from both of us. But only I was wide awake.

My chest began to pound—one beat, then two beats in the same second, faster and harder. For the first time in my life, I could feel the beats of my heart and the chill that snaked up my neck and delicately closed around my throat, making it hard to swallow.

Just as quickly as the pounding started, it subsided. Everything became quiet. As I lay—now detached from the warm body that had been so perfectly fitted to mine—a thought flashed through my mind as my eyelids began closing.

This could either be really, really good—or very bad.

Chapter 18

The Consequence

I stared at my bare feet and at the white floor beneath them. Everything around me was bright. Too bright. Past the rays of sunlight, a shadow was forming. I tried walking toward it, but my steps were slow and plodding, and it didn't get any clearer as I got closer. I picked up the pace— faster and faster, sprinting now—but I still wasn't closing the distance. I looked again at the floor and saw that it was moving in the opposite direction. It was like being on a treadmill; I was just running in place. I stopped, watching the shadowy entity disappear into the bright ray of light. I tried to call out, but when I opened my mouth to shout, no sound escaped.

I sat up in bed, choking for air.

Montana was awake, staring at me. "Petra," she huffed, then paused before asking, "Did we kiss last night?"

Her words shattered my ears like bullets, driving to the forefront of my mind a flashback of our lips touching, our legs coiling.

"Yeah." I blinked a couple times, trying to banish the thought from my head. I couldn't remember or understand why I had kissed her, and my heartbeat began to quicken. I lunged over her and off the bed, scanning the floor for my shoes. Quickly, I collected my things. "I need to go."

"Good idea," she said curtly.

I stopped, shocked at her tone. The tension rolled off her in waves.
She hates me.

I left her bedroom and ran quickly out the door, where the chilly air helped me to block out everything that had happened. Thankfully, I had class in less than an hour, and my classes kept me so busy that Montana and the kiss were erased from my mind for the whole day. I could only hope she had forgotten it as well.

When my last class was finally over, I hurried through the cold sleet toward my house, but stopped when I saw Montana standing by the commons, drenched. She must have been waiting for quite some time. I ran toward her, but upon catching a glimpse of the serious expression on her face, slowed down and walked cautiously the rest of the way.
"Hey! What are you doing here?"

She gave me a worried look. "Do you think we can walk . . . and talk?" she asked, shielding her eyes from the sleet.

Without waiting for a reply, she began to walk sullenly away. I followed like a puppy that had misbehaved.

"Petra," she said, turning around to face me at last, "that wasn't right. Last night. You don't do that." She turned and began to walk again.

It was not at all what I'd expected her to say. And I wasn't sure I liked *how* she said it, like it was my intention to mess with her.

"Taylor," I yelled. "I'm sorry." I ran in front of her, wanting her to see my face. "I did not intend to kiss you. I really don't remember how it even happened."

She recoiled. "You don't remember?"

"Don't worry." I tried to look into her eyes, which were hidden under her hair. "It didn't mean anything."

Her head shot up, and she finally looked into my eyes. Her expression was confused, as if she had a question but wasn't quite sure how to ask it.

"I was tired and wasn't thinking clearly," I continued. "It was a mistake."

I watched many different expressions ripple across her face as the minutes passed. *Does she need more reassurance?*

"We can't tell anyone about this," she finally said, terror in her voice.

"Of course," I assured her again. "Not a single person. No one will know."

She looked at me, blinking rapidly, until she finally relented and smiled.

"Okay then. See you, Petra," she said abruptly and quickly walked away.

I spent the rest of my walk home telling myself that she would be okay, but I couldn't help thinking that things weren't right. And in the next few days, I found how right I was.

∞

A week passed without me seeing or hearing from Montana. She substituted me for Britta and had been hanging out with her instead. In the second week, I began to feel a constant pressure on my chest that grew heavier with each passing day. I floated through each day, unaffected by and not invested in any of the events or conversations around me—yet totally affected by something else. Whenever I saw her on campus and tried to wave, I would get an I-don't-want-to-have-anything-to-do-with-you look, and then she would run quickly away in the opposite direction. I don't want to say I got used to that kind of reaction, but I began to expect it.

After one of those days, I walked home holding my chest, trying to push down the pressure. When I reached my house, I fell on top of my bed, not caring about the mud on my shoes, which I had trekked through the house. I didn't care about anything. The pressure in my chest was the worst it had ever been. It was excruciating.

I dove into my covers, throwing them over my head, and lay on my chest in hopes the ache would stop. It was throbbing, pumping through every vein and hitting every nerve in my body. The pressure was building and building, punching its way out harder and harder until finally I burst from under my covers, screaming while holding my injured chest. It could no longer take the pressure and suddenly exploded with a beam of light, like a flower blossoming toward the sun. I began to cry painfully, and my bed was soon soaked—in pain, in sorrow, in confusion, in joy—as every single emotion ever felt poured out of my now fully awakened heart.

It was pounding happily, beating ten times its normal pace. I couldn't believe it. I clutched my chest to feel the pounding within. *A heart?* I had to question it—I'd thought I had no such organ. I closed my eyes and took in the sound, hearing it echo in my ears and feeling it pump through my veins and vibrate off my skin. I sighed deeply and smiled. For the first time, I was feeling.

"How could this happen?" I cried out.

My heart was aching terribly, overwhelmed with emotion. I wrapped my arms around myself to contain it, but I still felt pain, happiness, sorrow, and fear. And lastly, I felt how helplessly despicable I was.

I lifted my hands and prayed to Cronus, asking him to rewind time and undo what had been done. My chest fought against my words, expanding even more. I held my arms tighter to my chest until finally, it all stopped.

Sensing Nick's ego, my heart had instantly closed tightly as if in hiding. Surprisingly, though, I was relieved to feel him coming.

The door swung open. The once flawless face was contorted with anguish.

"Nick, what's wrong?"

He hesitated, clearly deep in thought, for a long time before he got the words out. "I have to tell you something."

"What has happened to you?" I asked.

He wiped his forehead on his forearm, and I saw the scroll he was holding. "I have a message for you."

I nodded. "Yes?"

He slowly unraveled the scroll, and before reading, gave me an anxious look. "Petra Ambrosi, the Elders of Olympus regrettably inform you that the Moirai of the Heavens see your fate as unruly. Therefore, from this moment until further notice, you are to be reprimanded. Furthermore, all Lambdas will be suspended from the Heavens for the time being to await judgment by the Moirai." He leaned in and looked me squarely in the face. "I told you to be careful with your actions. I'll be seeing you."

He left before I could make sense of the message. That last part couldn't have been for me specifically, could it? I'm not a Lambda. I'm not one of The Enlightened.

I shook my head. The pressure in my chest began to rise again as my heartbeat raced and my nose began to tingle. I sped down the hall, turned the corner, and slammed into something hard. Britta flew down the other half of the hallway and hit the wall. My eyes widened when I saw her frightened face and felt her fear and confusion. Still, I ran past her and out the door. She called for me, but I was already running down the street, the wind whipping past my cheeks.

I found myself on a trail leading up the side of a huge mountain and followed it until it hugged a rocky front. I jumped on the rocks and began climbing, higher and higher, until I reached the top of a plateau where two large boulders faced the city below. I perched atop one of them and sat there until after the sun set, watching the sky turn from red to purple to blue—and then black. Virgo and Scorpio were the first constellations I spotted in the dark blanket above, and my mother's story echoed in my head.

The pressure in my chest was finally dissipating, and I started to feel normal again—feeling nothing. But questions still swirled in my mind. Where had the pressure come from? Was this how one became a Lambda? And would my chest open again, leaving my heart vulnerable?

My thoughts drifted to Montana—I had not spoken to her in three weeks. What was she feeling? Was her heart vulnerable, too?

Chapter 19

Allison Prome

I stood on the edge of a cliff, wanting to jump. In the distance, I saw the edge of another cliff, and on the other side, someone standing in a field of flowers. Warmth filled my chest. Instead of leaping straight down the cliff, I began making my way toward the land on the other side. The person there walked toward the other ledge and smiled, which gave me assurance that I would be caught if I fell.

Suddenly, a thick fog rose, and I could no longer see the person. The warmth turned cold, and the assurance was gone, replaced by fear, whispering words of doubt. I pondered whether to leap or not, moving up to and backing away from the ledge.

My feet slipped on the gravel beneath me; I lost my balance and staggered back, fearing the fall. It looked dark and deadly—lonely. I scooted back from the ledge, losing faith that I could make the leap, and no longer trusting that the person would be there to catch me—

I woke suddenly and climbed out of bed quickly—too quickly. My head felt unusually heavy from all the thoughts and dreams that were never released. I needed to free them somehow. I thought about going for a drive, but then I remembered I didn't have my truck.

I dressed in a hurry, not knowing why because I had nothing to do all day—no classes, no friends, no truck. Today would be a day just for me, then. I put my phone on the nightstand, left my room, and walked quickly down the hall.

Jaden was at the end of the hallway, and she grinned when she saw me. "Where are you going?"

"I'm not sure," I replied.

"For a run?"

I shrugged. "I don't really know."

She had me. I didn't know what I was doing and was still wondering why I felt the need to hurry.

"You can borrow my car if you need to use it, or my bike," she offered sweetly.

"Sure, thanks," I said. "Where's your bike?"

"In the garage. Help yourself."

In the garage, I scanned for the bike and spotted it in the corner, covered in carefully woven cobwebs. The metal handlebars and frame had corroded. I whisked away the delicate webs, grabbed one of the handles, and hopped onto the seat. The cold wind hit my face and cheeks like a block of ice as I steered down the driveway and began to pedal.

I took the same trail as the day before but climbed a different part of the mountain. I came upon a fork and decided to take the more treacherous one. The incline became steeper, and I pedaled harder, keeping my head down until I felt the ground underneath me begin to flatten. A cold breeze swarmed around me, and my violent shudders forced me to let go of the handlebars and hug my body. My heavy breathing had formed clouds of mist around me. I inhaled the thin Colorado air in a struggle to keep my muscles from tightening. But it was too late—I felt my hamstring clutch violently, and I fell to the ground. Physical pain? I had never felt it before. Something was changing.

"You cold?" a soft voice asked from behind me.

I didn't look. My muscles were still tightening. I waited for the sensation to subside, but to my surprise, it did not. The fog filled in around me, and my head fell in defeat.

"Freezing," I wheezed out.

Footsteps came closer, moving around my shivering body to stop in front of me. I looked up and eyed the figure, beginning with the feet. I scanned slowly up to her waist and spotted the Lambda brand proudly displayed on her tiny wrist. Her wrist was turned, exposing it clearly.

"You seem to recognize…" The voice faded out and I raised my head to see who it belonged to. I had to blink a couple of times before I realized that I recognized her. Her glow was too vibrant for Earth. And I was as familiar with her face as I was with her brand.

She stood a couple inches away from me. Her mahogany skin glowed just as it had the first time I'd seen her during the Ten-Day Celebration. It was the Goddess with the purple and silver wreaths, one of those who had hidden their hands in handmade pockets. She fixed her glowing, caramel eyes on me, examining me, and then lit up as if remembering something.

"You're Petra, right?" she asked exuberantly. I nodded.

"I've heard about you," she said, smiling. "You're Taylor's friend, right?"

My body warmed up at the sound of her name, and suddenly my muscles started to loosen. I was able to stand up, and I dusted myself off while eyeing her suspiciously.

Aside from her unnerving question, it was a bit odd to see her at the top of the mountain, wearing clothes from the Heavens. She took a couple steps toward me.

" I'm Allison . . . Allison Prome." She put her hand out to me.

I stared at her wrist, eyeing the brand and nearly forgetting to shake. As I fitted my hand into hers, a rush of adrenaline came galloping at me, through me. I pulled my hand back quickly, as if she had shocked me, but the adrenaline lingered in my hand, tingling my fingertips.

"Nice to meet you." My voice cracked. "Do I know you?"

"I've seen you around." She paused. "Here at Regis and in the Heavens. "

I nodded. "How do you know Taylor?"

"It's a small school." She smiled. "She and her roommates are good friends of mine."

Good friends? Could that mean Montana knew about us?

"Do they know—?"

"Know I'm a Lambda?" she asked, giggling. "Yeah, but they don't—"

"No, no." I stopped her before she continued, though I wished I hadn't—I think I would have liked to hear her answer. "I meant do they know you're from the Heavens?"

Her eyes lit up instantly. "No," she said abruptly. "The souls who bore that secret would be ruined."

I felt that to be dishearteningly true.

"But they know you're a Lambda?" I asked.

"Yes." Her face perked up. "But here, they use a more insolent word. You'll probably hear it around sooner
or later." My eyes met hers.
"What's the word?"

"You'll know it when they say it by how they say it—the way it comes off their tongue so sharp and bold, while the underlying tone screams disappointment."

She walked slowly around me, still looking down. Then I felt her anger rise.

"And as they hold the last letter tightly with their teeth, it will be as if time pauses until it is let go from their tongue. Once time is released from its pause, the judgment will come." Her words burned like coals, feeding her anger. "You'll feel it the moment the word departs their mouth."

I coughed out a cold breath. "Who's worse at judging?" I asked. "Earth or the Heavens?"

She looked at me, silent for a time, then nodded and beckoned me to follow her. She climbed onto the huge boulder I had perched on the night before and rested her chin in her hand as if pondering.

"This is not reality," she said finally. "Here there is nothing to worry about. Mortals are naïve and sheltered by the traditions man has created. However, the Heavens are reality. It is home." She paused. "At least, it used to be, but things have changed. Over the past couple of decades, the Heavens have become like the mortals 'world." She raised her hand and lifted her pointer finger to the clouds above. "They want us to live like them." She laughed. "Equal my ass," she spat.

I felt the hairs on my arms stand up, not from the chilly temperature, but from her passion. Allison Prome's thoughts echoed some of my own. I found myself hypnotized by her truth. It was true—there was no equality in being branded and then banished from home.

"Is that why you're here on the mountain top?" I asked. I found myself mesmerized, waiting for her to speak.

"We are all here on Earth now. It's to be our holding cell," she said. "We were kicked out of the Heavens. Literally! They came into our homes, our training classes—everywhere—and kicked us out!" Her voice rose with fury. "I have never felt so betrayed by my own kind."

"Who kicked you out?" I wondered aloud.

"The Horai and the Heavens' Guards," she said, shaking her head.

I could not believe the Horai were visible—I had been led to believe they were spirits. "The Horai had skin?"

She laughed. "Yeah! And I thought they weren't even real!" I laughed with her. "Me too!"

"And they were beautiful. I've never seen tainted Goddesses look so innocent. They glowed like the three morning stars and wore robes as white as freshly fallen snow. Their eyes were white gold, and each had long, flowing hair. The middle one had red curls, the older one wavy auburn hair, and the youngest, golden locks."

Again, I was mesmerized, imagining what the Horai looked like. We sat in silence for a while, staring at the town below.

"So what are you going to do now?" I asked softly.

"Find a place to live," she said with a sigh. "I used to share an apartment near campus with my girlfriend, but after we broke up, I went back to my home in the Heavens." Laughing, she added, "There's no way in Hades my ex would let me stay with her. My only other option is to ask Taylor, Sade, and Tawny if I could stay with them." She fell quiet, thinking. "I should go ask them now." She got up from the rock, turning to face me. "Want to come?"

I thought about the expression on Montana's face when she saw me walk through their door—the same expression I had been seeing for three weeks. I shook my head. "No thanks."

She shrugged. "Alright then. I guess I'll see you around."

Chapter 20

April's Showers

Two months had passed since the kiss, and Montana still hadn't responded to a single text or call. I had concluded that our friendship was over. Thankfully, I'd been blessed with new company. The free time I'd once spent with Montana had been transferred to Jaden, who had helped change my sleepless nights into nights of parties and sporting events.

One night, Jaden, Jessica, Diane, and I headed to a party. As I entered the gigantic house, the floodgates of emotions opened and flowed. It was just as bad as it had been at the hospital. But this time, pain and grief were replaced by lust and desire as co-eds chatted each other up.

I needed some peace, so I went outside looking for somewhere to sit. Although it was dark, I noticed Allison Prome sitting with someone at the nearest table. I felt no urgency to talk to her, and I sensed she and her partner were having a serious discussion, so I tried to make my way past them unnoticed.

"Petra?" *Too late.* Allison was waving at me. I raised my hand slowly and gave her a faint wave back. Feeling anger from her companion, I hurried to a neighboring table, sitting with my back facing them, but I heard Allison coming over. I closed my eyes and felt more anger.

Allison sat on the other side of the table. "Hey, Petra," she said, smiling, "it's good to see you again."

" What are you doing here?" I asked, and then glanced over my shoulder, still feeling her friend's irritation.

"We're leaving soon." She eyed the person behind me.

"Ally, let's go," her friend said.

"Alright, give me a minute." I felt her friend's burning eyes on me, and then she stomped angrily away toward the house.

"She probably thinks I'm hitting on you," Allison said. "Remember the ex-girlfriend I was telling you about?"

I nodded.

"Well, that's her."

I swung my head back toward the house, but the girl was nowhere in sight. "You guys still hang out together?"

"Yeah." Allison shrugged. "She's my best friend. I still love her."

I watched Allison carefully. I could sense she held onto her ex. She was still smiling but stopped once she noticed me staring.

"I'll see you around," she said and left.

I was finally alone—in peace. I closed my eyes and envisioned myself on my island, my sanctuary. I was getting deep into my meditation when I felt the table move. I opened my eyes to find Montana sitting in front of me. She wasn't looking at me.

"Hey," she finally said. "How've you been?"

How've I been? Well, let's see—the one person I was closest to pushed me away, so I've been great. Not!
"Good," I said aloud. "How about you?"

She looked at me. "I'm good, thanks," she said curtly, brushing the question aside. "Were you just talking to Allison Prome?"

Two months, and she breaks her silence to ask me that?
I nodded.

"Why?" Her tone was ugly.

"Why?" I asked. "Do you prohibit her from speaking to me, too?"

"How do you know her?" she shot back.

"I just met her." My voice began to rise in volume.

"Was she hitting on you?" she asked rudely.

"No!"

"It looked like she

Was."was this a

Joke?
"We were just talking," I snapped.

"Well it didn't look like it."

I slammed my hands on the table and stood up. "You haven't spoken to me in forever, and this is what you want to talk about?" My stomach and chest began to twist and burn.
Her face fell. "I–I've been busy," she said, her voice finally gentle. "I'm sorry."

I leaned in over
the table. "Busy?"
"Y-Yeah, I've been
busy."
I said nothing, but shook my head and then sat back down. What was she hiding?

We sat in silence for a couple minutes, but it seemed like forever.
"What are you doing tomorrow?" she finally asked.

I shrugged and shook my head.

"Do you want to hang out?" she asked softly.

"Oh, you won't be busy?"

"No," she answered and rolled her eyes.

I had planned what I would say to her if given the chance. I wanted to yell and scream at her. I wanted to curse her for what she had put me through and for what she had caused to happen to me. But I didn't do any of that. What I had planned blew away with the winter wind as soon as I saw her smile.

"Okay then," I said.

∞

Apria's sapphire eyes were weary and saddened. Her glow was brighter than usual—beautiful and perfect. It was sickening to most Deities who gazed upon her, but to me she was the best creation—more spectacular than any mortal or immortal could imagine. Perfection stared me in the face, and all I could do was smile back. A tear formed in her right eye—just one.

"Why are you crying?" I asked. Was it her beauty that made her cry?

"I lost you," she whispered sadly. "You'll never remember."

Loud music began playing as I stared at her with confusion, and I woke up from my dream to the same loud tune coming from Britta's room. She had forgotten to turn off her alarm when she left for the weekend. It was seven o'clock. I wanted to fall back asleep to discover what Apria had meant. I walked into Britta's room and slammed my hand down on the radio to silence it. The music stopped, and I dragged my feet back toward my own room. I was in the hallway when I heard the front door open. I turned to see who it was, and Jessica Eris came around the corner with a big smile painted on her face. Quickly after our soccer season had ended, she'd started dating someone, and I had barely seen her since.

She grabbed me and gave me a huge hug. "What are you up to, lady?"

"Sleeping" I said, rubbing my eyes. "What are you up to?" "Haven't seen you in a while, so I thought I'd stop by." "This early?" I asked.

"Oh, well, you know, I'm an early riser."

I'd never thought that about her. During our first week of three-a-days she was always the sleepy one. This was the first time I'd felt a lie from Jessica, and I had no clue why she had any reason to be dishonest. But I had an eerie feeling she hadn't woken up at dawn just to see how I'd been.

She stepped back and looked at me with a fake smile. "What do you have planned today?"

"I'm hanging out with Taylor," I said with a big yawn.

"With Taylor?" she started nodding. "Cool. Still think she's immortal?" she asked playfully.

"Ha, ha. I don't know. This will be the first time we've hung out in a while. She kinda disappeared on me."

"Disappeared?" she asked, more inquisitive than ever.

"Yeah, I don't know." I walked back into my room and plopped on the bed. "Speaking of disappearing, what have you been up to lately?"

She followed me to the bed and sat down. "Oh, just busy."

"That seems to be the thing these days," I muttered.

"Yeah, busy with school and the boyfriend. Speaking of!" She hopped up. "I'm meeting him for breakfast." She began to walk out. "Nice seeing you, Pei. See ya around!"

And with that, she disappeared down the hall, leaving me wondering what the hell that was about.

∞

Montana pulled up to my house in a car I had never seen her drive before. The windows were darkly tinted, and I could barely make out her shadow. I quickly ran to the car and hopped in, slamming the door behind me.

I turned to her and smiled. "Hey."

She put the car into drive without saying a word, and without even a hint of a smile.

"So where are we going?" I asked, breaking the silence.

"I'm starving, so we're going to the market," she said curtly. Her tense grip on the steering wheel was a bit frightening.

I couldn't feel her, as usual, but my tension began to build. With every passing second of silence, it grew bigger, until I finally asked, "What's wrong with you?"

Her eyes fluttered and her body jerked uncomfortably. "Nothing," she said sharply, deceptively.

"Then why are you acting . . ." I wanted to choose my words carefully, but why should I care after the way she'd been treating me? "Rude. You're being very rude," I said and then sulked in my seat.

Without looking at me or saying a word, she pulled off to the side of the road and shut off the engine.

"You told Allison Prome you wanted to hang out?" She didn't look at me directly.

"Wh-What? Hang out?"

"She said she was going to hang out with you. Like a date, Petra!"

"You're joking, right?" The air felt thick and stuck in my throat. What was she feeling? "I never said anything about hanging out with anyone."

She leaned on the armrest and hesitated before answering. "I thought you wanted this," she said, still refusing to look at me in the eye.

I leaned over the armrest as well, closer to her, and shook my head slowly as I tried to meet her aqua eyes. "No, Taylor. I definitely did not."

She finally turned her head and looked at me. Her face was close to mine, and I could feel her throat relaxing, see her chest rising and then falling gently. She stared into my eyes and at my lips, then hesitated. I watched her lean in. Her eyes closed, and she breathed slowly. After a moment, she opened her eyes and stared back into mine.

"Okay," she whispered. She sat up and started the car.

I couldn't believe what had happened. It was another first. I couldn't explain what I'd just felt, and what I'd wanted her to do. What would have happened if she had leaned in even closer?

∞

The day went by quickly, as time always did when hanging out with Montana. I didn't realize how late it was or how tired I felt until I laid down on my bed and stared at the empty ceiling. Before my eyelids could close, the doorbell rang. I didn't move to answer it. *Jaden will get it*. Suddenly, I felt an electrical surge rush through the wooden floorboards, down the hallway, underneath me, and up through my toes. My body jumped as the surge tickled the bottoms of my feet and crawled up my legs, to my stomach, and then to my chest. The bedroom door opened slowly, and Allison stepped in, stinking of liquor. Her power was so strong. I thought that if I were to touch her, I would most certainly explode.

Before I could say a word, she grabbed my hand.

"We need to talk," she said quickly and led me out of the house.

As we walked into the night, I felt her excitement about something. She was tiny, the top of her head several inches below my eyes, so I looked down at her and waited for her to speak. She started to say something but stopped, and then began walking down the sidewalk. I followed.

"Can you walk on the street?" she asked. "I don't like you towering over me."

I laughed and stepped off the sidewalk.

"So I'm just wondering," she began, "are you and Taylor . . . talking or something?"

I stopped walking to look at her, sense her—to see if she was joking. "Talking?" I asked. "As in dating?"

106

She smiled and nodded. "Yeah. She was quite upset about . . . something."

My jaw hung open. "About what?"

"I told her that . . . I was going to try . . ." she put her head down and smiled, "to kiss you tonight."

I recoiled immediately. "I'm sorry?" I asked. "And why would you tell her that?"

"What? You don't want that?" She wasn't offended—she had way too much confidence for that—but she was surprised, as if she had never been turned down before.

"Allison, I'm not . . . I don't . . . I'm not like that," I said.

"So you're saying you've never kissed a girl before?"

I fell back in step with her, chuckling. "Um, no . . . I ha—"

"I know you have," she said, smiling boastfully.

"How do you know?"

"Taylor told me last night."

"She what?" I felt my muscles tighten beneath my skin.

Allison kept talking, but I was beyond hearing. Questions began forming. What was this feeling? What was the word? I had never experienced it personally before. *Betrayal?* Montana had told someone.

Underneath those thoughts were even more questions, as well as a slither of excitement. Was I feeling Allison, or were those my feelings? I became confused about how to decipher the difference as thoughts ran mean cycles around my mind.

"Why are you upset she told me?" I heard someone ask—I had forgotten Allison was standing there.

"Because it was an accident! I didn't mean to kiss her. It just . . . happened. I didn't—We didn't want anyone to know." I walked quickly now, my thoughts racing. Why was I upset? Why was I excited? What did this mean?

Allison followed me. Her small, quick steps were surprisingly well matched to my long strides.

"So why do you think she told me?"

I stopped and looked at her, sensing she already knew the answer. It was not a question for her, but a question for me to ask myself. "I don't know. You guys are friends?"

"I think she's not as uncomfortable with it as you are." She smiled. "Maybe she even liked it." Her smile grew wider.

I felt my eyes roll—I didn't like what she was saying. She was putting thoughts in my head—more thoughts. What if she *had* liked it? Had I liked it, too?

"That's what made me think you guys were talking. She got really upset when I told her I wanted to try to kiss you." She stopped and waited for me to say something, but I kept my head down and tried to focus on my steps and not on her words. "She's the one who dropped me off and quickly sped away. It was weird, now that I think about it," she said, talking more to herself now than to me. "I shouldn't have come," she added sincerely. "I could have gotten you into trouble."

"Why?" I asked.

She kept her head down. "Because I think Sade, Tawny, my ex, and Taylor now think that you might be interested in me."

Something happened to me as I heard her words. Normally, words would never cause any emotion in me. I might even laugh at the valiant attempt, or try to pretend that I cared. However, the mention of Montana got to me. I didn't want to inflict any pain on her. At that moment, I cared. I didn't like to think of Montana angry, especially if what she was angry at was false. I did not want to kiss Allison. I didn't want to be with Allison at all. I wanted to go talk to Montana.

My mouth was dry from breathing in too much air. My chest felt heavy, and my tongue stuck to the sides of my mouth.

"What did they say?" I finally asked.

"I was boasting," she said. "A lot. I was telling them I could get you by the end of the night."

"Wow." I gasped. She sounded like the old me.

"Yeah, my ex wasn't too happy about that. Neither was Tay."

"Allison . . ." I felt my blood heating up beneath my skin. I tried to relax, but I wanted to scream at her. I was shocked at the cockiness that had driven her to come to me. The sudden temperature change within my body was giving me a headache. I pressed my knuckles into my forehead.

"I'm sorry," she said. "I think Ashton and Tay might really hate you now. I'm really sorry, Petra. Ashton told me not to come—she said I'd scare you."

The aching began to subside some, and I kept walking, making her follow me. "Who is Ashton?"

"My ex."

Ashton? Could it be the same Ashton that Taylor had said I resembled? "Please don't say anything more about this, or about what happened between me and Taylor," I said, shaking my head.

"I won't. Just don't tell Ashton you rejected me."

I wondered why that would matter. I wanted to ask, but then realized I didn't really care to know, so I kept quiet. It was getting later and colder. "You ready to go home now?" I asked.

"Yeah, let me call Tay to come pick me up." She reached for her phone and started dialing.

I waited, looking up at the clear night sky and the stars. The suburban streetlamps were dimly lit, so I was still able to take in the whole sky. It was nothing like the sight from the Heavens, though it was still pretty.

"She's not picking up," she said.

I looked down the street and noticed we had walked halfway from my house to the school. "We're almost there anyway. We can just walk."

We reached the Residence Village and entered Montana's apartment building, where Allison let us in.

"You're staying here, right?" I asked.

Allison looked at her phone and shook her head. "No, Ashton wants me to come over."

"Okay then. Have a good night. Thanks for coming over," I said, chuckling.

"Umm, I don't have a car. Ashton lives off campus."

"I don't have a car either," I said.

"Ask Tay?"

"You ask her," I said.

"No, you," she said, pushing me down the hallway toward her bedroom. She was right behind me as I slowly opened Montana's door and saw her cozily tucked in bed. The grey moon lit up her face. I lingered, just watching her. She looked stunning—so peaceful.

Allison stormed past me. "Tay! Tay! Wake up!"

Montana jumped up quickly, and her eyes caught mine. Immediately, I regretted being there. Her shocked expression quickly turned angry. She turned to Allison.

"What, Ally?"

"We need to use your jeep. I'm staying at Ashton's tonight."

Montana looked at me, and then at Allison, and then back to me. "Are you going with her?"

I winced. "No, I'm dropping her off, and then I'll bring your car back."

She seemed surprised. "Okay, but I swear, Brosi, if you scratch my jeep, I'm going to kill you."

I would love to see you try. " I promise," I said through a smile.

Ashton lived only five minutes away down the main street, and I soon pulled up to the curb.

"This one right here?"

Allison nodded, looking out the window distractedly as if waiting for something. I didn't know whether to speak or let her be, so I put the car in park and waited. She finally looked back at me, realizing I was still there.

"Thanks for driving me," she said.

"Sure," I told her. "Thanks again for this adventurous night."

She reached over to unfasten her seatbelt. "Yeah, sorry about all that."

She got out and I drove the jeep back. I crept into Montana's room to return her keys and was almost out the door when I heard her speak. "Petra? Where are you going?"

I turned around and saw her head poking out over the covers. She sounded so sweet, so vulnerable.

"I'm walking home. Your car keys are on your end table."

"You're leaving? It's cold out. You'll get sick."

I never get sick. "It's not a problem," I said, but without knowing why, I began heading back to her, in the opposite direction of where I should have been going.

"So did you guys kiss?" she
asked bluntly. I laughed. "No."

Even in the darkness, I saw

her face relax.

"Do you like her?" she asked
                    sadly.

My muscles tightened, and my heart started to beat faster. I concentrated and tried to slow it down. Then I took in a deep breath. "No," I said, staring directly into her eyes so she could see my sincerity.

Finally, she began to smile. That was all my heart needed to relax. I let out my breath and she breathed it in. For that single moment, we were sharing air, sharing heartbeats, drinking in each other's energy. I couldn't let go of her—and that frightened me.

"I should go," I said aloud and began to turn away, but she gently grabbed my wrist.

"Don't," she whispered. "Just stay . . . please."

Her request was too gentle to answer coldly. My feet were cemented to the ground. "For how long?"

"Until you want to leave." Her velvet voice was all it took to get me to stay. I nodded slowly, took off my shoes, and hopped over her to where I had slept the last time.

I tucked myself under the covers and she scooted away from me, closer to the edge of the bed, and turned her back to me. I just watched her, trying to sense anything I could. What was she thinking? The thought danced in my head as I drifted off to sleep.

Chapter 21

New Beginnings

Persephone, the daughter of Demeter, Goddess of the Harvest, was out in the garden one day. She was a young and beautiful maiden at the time, full of love and light, and Hades, the God of Death and the Underworld, saw her and became captivated. He had to have her, so he brought her to his underworld kingdom.

Demeter searched the Heavens and the Earth for Persephone but could not find her. Heartbroken, Demeter had no life to give to the Earth's harvest anymore, which caused a terrible drought. Humans suffered and starved and could not offer any sacrifices to the Gods. Because of this, Zeus became angry and went to talk to his brother, Hades, into returning Persephone to her mother. Ultimately, Hades gave in—but not without conditions.

The Moirai tell us that if anyone eats or drinks anything from the Underworld, that person will have to remain for a specified time period. So, Hades tricked Persephone into eating six pomegranate seeds. Because she had done so, she was forced to stay in the Underworld for six months of each year. The other six months could be spent with her mother.

And so, every six months, Persephone returns to the Underworld, leaving her mother devastated and in a depression, which all of Earth shares with her. But when Persephone returns to Demeter, Demeter in turn blesses the Earth and the humans with the most bountiful harvest.

Persephone's story was one of my favorites growing up—the story of the cycle of life. We live, we die, and we are reborn. There is always a beginning and an end—and then a beginning again. Nothing is forever. Everything is temporary.

I knew the day Persephone was released from the Underworld and reunited with her mother—the day that marked a beginning. I felt it. I could sense Persephone's essence everywhere. A warm breeze blew and spun around me, its delicate fingers on my chin, lifting my head to see the sun's shadow behind a sheet of grey clouds. It smelled like rain, yet not one drop had fallen. What was Demeter waiting for?

I wanted to stay outside all day, affixed to the big boulder on the mountain. But I had papers to write and homework to do. I hated mortal school and the content it taught—all of it was so unnecessary.

I entered the library and felt everyone instantly, all at once. As much as it annoyed me to enter a building filled with mortals, I also somewhat enjoyed sensing what went on inside them. The boy at the front desk was enticed by whatever book he was reading, but the boy sitting directly next to him was bored with his. I walked toward the computers, passing rows and rows of books, and saw a girl stressing over a project.

Another girl walked timidly toward a basketball player, and the basketball player timidly welcomed her. She liked him. They liked each other. That made me smile.

As I reached the computers, the students around me were surprisingly calm and stress-free—for now at least, until finals started. When that happened, I didn't want to be anywhere near the library. It would be worse than the hospital.

I spotted Montana in the back of the library, sitting at a desk. There was an empty seat next to her, so I walked over and set my things down on it. She lifted her head from her huge textbook and smiled.

"Hey!" I whispered loudly.

"Hi," she whispered back. "Do you have a lot of homework?" I nodded.

"Well, hurry up and get started."

I laughed quietly. "Yes, ma'am."

When I finally reached the conclusion of my twelve-page biology paper, I glanced over at Montana. She was deep in thought, lip-reading her text, and then rereading it, committing the words to memory. I found it humorous . . . and cute.

She looked up from her book and caught my gaze. "What?"

My mind went blank, and I forgot what I was doing. "Um, are you done yet?" I spat out dumbly.

"Yeah, just rereading."

My eyes focused on her biting her bottom lip.

"Are you hungry?" she asked.

I nodded and jumped up quickly, shaking off my trance. "Yeah, let's get something to eat."

We left the library and started walking to the student center.

"Did you finish your homework?" she asked.

"Yes, I did."

She smiled. "Good. Because tonight we're going out . . . with Ashton." I stopped walking. Suddenly, I was no longer hungry. "Ashton? Allison's ex? The girl who hates me?"

She laughed. "Yeah. Her," she said nonchalantly as she walked past me.

It was not the reassurance I had expected. "But why?" I sped up to catch up with her. "Does she know I'm coming?"

"Yes," she said, still chuckling.

"What's so funny?"

"Your reaction."

I could not see her face but could tell she was still smiling.

"Hey, AJ!" she called out as she ran toward a student. I watched as she reached up and gave the girl a big hug. I could not help thinking about what might happen hanging out with a girl who hated me.

"Petra, this is Ashton."

I looked up from the pavement and saw her. *Wow*. She was beautiful.

Ashton's eyes were like lariats, roping me in unwillingly. They were big and blue like the brightest sky, and she had dark brown hair that fell over her high cheekbones. I didn't know how long her hand had been held out because I was still wrapped up in her eyes. I only noticed it when she looked down. My eyes followed, and I reached out to shake her hand. My fingers touched her palm, and with that action a burst of emotion rushed through my tendons. She flinched with me, and we both let go instantly. Had she felt it too?

It was the weirdest thing I'd felt since kissing Montana. My gaze darted between them as Montana watched me and Ashton smiled back curiously. Something changed then. The grey clouds suddenly let go, and it started sprinkling, the rain fueling the adrenaline rushing through me. It was coming from the both of them—no, all three of us.

"So you're Petra." She grinned.

"I am."

I was still struck by what had happened, and still drawn by her eyes. I decided to smile back. She looked harmless, but felt deadly.

"Are you going out with us tonight?"

I hesitated. "Do you want me to?" I asked, staring directly into her eyes.

She laughed. What a beautiful laugh.

"Absolutely." She flashed me a charming smile.

∞

When Montana picked me up that night, I opened the passenger door and was greeted by her welcoming smile. Climbing in, I was immediately warmed by her.

"You ready for tonight?" she asked with a big grin.

"Surrre," I said sarcastically.

We arrived at the bar on Main Street, the locals 'favorite hangout. It had a small but sufficient dance floor with a slightly elevated lounge looking over it. When you walked in, there was a small bar to the left, and tucked away in the right corner was an area for shuffleboard and darts. Ashton was standing at the bar, flirting with the male bartender.

We walked over and sat down next to her. Ashton hadn't noticed we were there—she was still flirting with the bartender—so Montana turned to me and put her hand on my thigh, gently.

"Be right back—I'm going to go to the restroom," she yelled, projecting her voice over the loud music. I nodded. Even after she left, I could still feel the warmth on my thigh from where her hand had been. I turned to face the shelves of bottles, staring at the flat-screen TV. I sighed and rolled my eyes when I saw the movie playing: *Shipwreck.*

"You need anything, hun?" asked the gorgeous, muscle-bound man behind the bar.

"A glass of merlot, please?" I yelled back.

He eyed me skeptically. "Can I see some ID?" *Damn.* I still didn't have my license. "I don't have it." "Then sorry, hun," he said. I smiled politely. "Water is fine."

He stared back at me, and his smile faded. "No problem."

"Hey."

I turned to Ashton. She was wearing a black leather jacket and a charming grin and holding a mug. She leaned against the bar. "So I have a question—"

Before she could finish, I cut her off—I already knew what she was going to ask. "No, I did not do anything with her."

She leaned in closer, and her grin grew wider. "—Do you want to be my shuffleboard partner?" she asked.

I looked at her, slightly embarrassed. My assumption had been wrong, and so I smiled at her. She laughed.

"Oh," I said, laughing with her.

"But thanks for . . ." she paused and looked me up and down, ". . . letting me know." She winked and smiled again.

I got up from the bar and looked to the corner where the shuffleboards were. "I don't know how to play."

She finally stood up, smiling at me. My eyes caught at her lips as she spoke. "I'll teach you."

After Ashton and I lost the game because of my inability to toss well, we made our way back to a part of the bar overlooking the dance floor. I immediately noticed Montana dancing with some guy. Looking closer, I noticed it was Trent, our hot young soccer coach. After the song ended, Montana whispered something in his ear. He laughed, and she left him to join us at the bar. I did not mention Trent to her, although I really wanted to.

Jaden and Diane met up with us halfway through the night, and we crashed the dance floor together. At one point, I thought I saw Nick in the corner, but when I was able to get a good enough look, there was no one there. Must have been the strobe lights messing with my eyes.

When the bar closed, we all tumbled out to the parking lot and piled into Montana's jeep. It was a full car now. Our first stop was Ashton's apartment. She hopped out with Montana and walked to her front door, but then they disappeared inside while the three of us waited in the jeep. They both came back out and hopped into the car. Ashton carried her folded pajamas in her arms.

"Ashton is going to spend the night at your place. If that's cool." I turned and looked at Montana. *Why?* My head became jumbled with confusion.

"Is that okay?" Montana asked, staring hard at me.

Was she threatening me or asking me? I stared back at her, extremely curious about what she was thinking. I found myself scared to say no. "Sure," I muttered.

Montana stopped at our house, and we all got out of the car. Jaden and Diane raced up to the front door, and Ashton followed them. I held onto the passenger door, looking at Montana. *Why?* I wanted to ask, but said nothing.

"Have fun," Montana said, giving me a fake smile, then motioned me to close the door. It felt like I had been smacked. Was she joking?

I walked into my house slowly, still absorbed in my thoughts. Why would Montana have Ashton spend the night with me? I looked up to see Ashton sitting on the couch, smiling.

"Did you want me to sleep on the couch?" she asked.

"I don't care," I mumbled. What the heck was wrong with Montana? I sat down near Ashton, overwhelmingly confounded.

"I'm sorry. I didn't mean for you to get stuck with me. Tay offered, and I thought you wanted a sleepover. I thought she was going to join, too." Her explanation confused me even more, but I didn't ask for clarification.

"It's just weird," I muttered.

"Maybe she thought we should talk . . . since, you know . . . I do hate you."

I smiled back but did not find it nearly as funny as she did.

The warmth of Montana's car had disappeared, and I felt the frozen grip of the house take hold of my body. Without saying a word, I walked down the hallway and into my bedroom, still in a daze, wishing Montana would appear in front of me and tell me what she was thinking. Ashton followed behind me.

I went into the bathroom to change, and after switching clothes, I leaned over the sink, staring at the running faucet. *If only I could read minds. If only I could read hers.* I shook the thoughts from my head and splashed my face with some water.

I walked back into my bedroom and found Ashton already underneath the covers. I lifted the comforter and eased myself under as well, laying my head down and closing my eyes. I felt her eyes on me.

"Do I scare you or something?" she asked. "I don't bite."

I turned my head to find her leaning over me, grinning through the darkness.

"No. Why?"

Her grin grew bigger. "Just wondering." She stayed there for a bit before laying back down. "Petra Ambrosi, where on Earth did you come from?"

What do you mean?" I asked.

"It's a pretty small school. I'd never heard of you or seen you before. And then one night, this girl—out of nowhere—is talking to Allison." She plopped her head back down on the pillow. "And that mystery girl makes so much of an impression on her that she comes to her house, wanting to be with her." She turned her head to look at me. "So who is this mystery girl?"

I held my tongue as she continued to watch me.

"How did you and Allison meet?" I asked. I thought it was a skillful topic change and wondered if she knew that Allison was a Goddess.

She laughed, and I realized I really liked her laugh. In it, I could feel her edge, her excitement—every tiny hair standing straight on her arms. It was a beautiful sound.

"I actually met her at my boyfriend's party," she said, still chuckling.

"Your boyfriend?" She had my attention now.

"Yeah. Ha. I was sitting on his lap at his house party, and she saw me, walked up to me, and started hitting on me—right in front of him. I thought she was crazy." She got lost in her own thoughts for a moment. "But her confidence was extremely sexy to me." She paused again and bit her lip—seductively. "We started dating shortly after that night."

I smiled sadly. Her story had taken me back to times I didn't want to remember. That was who I was at Gaianus—a reckless Goddess who used her gifts to torture, who was disconnected from emotion. But that was not who I wanted to be at Regis. I shook my head in disgrace. Regis was a new place, a new school—a new beginning.

"Petra, are you asleep?"

I came back to the present to find Ashton's face close to mine. Her skin was flawless and glowed in the moon's light. She looked like a Goddess.

"Sorry," I said, still shaking the memory from my head. "Why did you and Allison break up?"

"Well . . ." She laid back down, resting her head on the pillow and staring at the ceiling. "We were unhealthy." She paused. "We fought a lot. We held different values," she said, but then stopped again. "I can't believe I just told you all that." I shifted my attention from the blank ceiling to Ashton's face. "*Why* did I even tell you that?" she asked. "And why am I the only one talking?"

I smiled at her. "Because I'm listening."

Suddenly, there was a loud sound from my end table. My phone.

Montana?

"Are you going to get that?"

Yes was my first thought, but *why would she be texting me* was my second. My heart began pulsating in my chest. *Why am I reacting like this?* I felt the heat of my body rise, and the anger drip in my blood. *Why didn't she stay with me tonight?*

"No. I'm not going to get it. It's fine. Where do you come from?" I turned my head away from the end table and back to Ashton's grin.

"I'm from California. Near Angeles National Forest? Nowhere near the city. You?"

California. Not the Heavens. I guess she wasn't a Goddess.

Another vibration sounded, and we both looked in the direction of the sound. It was coming from the pile of Ashton's clothes on the floor.

"You going to get that?" I said, smiling as I mocked her earlier words. Then I sat up. "What if it's Allison?"

"Wow, calm down, tiger," she said, and then put her hand on my shoulder. I could sense her intentions in her warmth. "She's probably wondering if I'm coming home."

"You should get it," I said, sounding a little too eager.

"Why?" She moved her hand from me. "You're scared?"

"Not possible," I teased.

"Oh, yeah?" She raised her eyebrows and slowly moved closer to me, skimming my lips with hers. "How about now?" Her lips teased mine, brushing against them as she spoke. I felt her heart pounding loudly, echoing mine, screaming for my lips.

I remained quiet, trying to ignore her blood boiling with excitement. She moved her bottom lip again, and this time it brushed even more firmly against mine. I held still and closed my eyes. I wanted to disappear inside myself, and yet she pulled me in closer.

May the blade of inquiry stab me for what is about happen.

I moved my lips with hers, the softest lips I had ever kissed. Why did they have to feel so good against mine? So sweet, so innocent. Yet, at the same time, not so innocent.

I pushed her away and turned from her. "I can't believe I just did that," I whispered.

I felt her worry instantly. "Petra, I'm sorry."

I looked at the door. I should make a run for it—go to Montana.

"I just freaked you out, didn't I?" She moved away from me, and I felt guilt drift through her. Guilt's hands wrapped around me as well, pushing me into a well of shame.

117

"No," I said. "You didn't freak me out."

But I had freaked myself out, for I realized I enjoyed it. I enjoyed it more than I thought I ever could. This time I was completely sober, my emotions beating awake—feeling. It was a new beginning. I had taken a bite of the forbidden apple, and it tasted sweet.

Chapter 22

Paranoia's Sweet Kiss

The sunrise colored the sky tangerine, and a noble yellow crept over it, threatening to swallow the reds and oranges. I stared out my window and watched my parents out in the fields, picking the ripened peaches. A dark figure caught my eye two rows away from them and I squinted, making out a young man with dark curly hair, wearing a fedora. He raised his arm and pointed at me.

I felt the bed shake and opened my eyes just in time to see Ashton leap over me and dive toward her clothes. She raced to put them on as she struggled to hold the phone to her ear.

"What are you doing?" I asked, blinking to focus.

Ashton covered the phone's receiver. "Allison is picking me up now. She's right around the corner." She kept hopping as she tried to get her legs into her jeans. I looked at the clock. It was 6:30 in the morning. A sudden rush of fear ran through me. Was I in trouble? I couldn't help but think that I was, that I had done a bad thing. But then again, I had no reason to think that. I wasn't involved with anyone—I could kiss whomever I wanted. But I had kissed a girl . . . *another* one. And I *was* in trouble . . . with the Moirai.

"Why is she coming?" I asked when Ashton finally hung up the phone.

She hopped on the other foot as she pulled on a shoe. "I guess Tay was texting her last night, saying 'Ashton is spending the night with Petra, and they might be doing something. 'She kept asking Allison if she was upset. Allison didn't seem to care, but Tay sure did." She stopped hopping and smiled at me. I shot her a look and then jumped out of bed.

I *was* in trouble. I grabbed clothes and threw them on quickly. By the time I finished, Ashton was headed to the front door. Before she reached it, she turned around and looked at me—without her grin.

"Hey, listen, I'm sorry for last night. I understand if you don't want to talk to me anymore." She started to turn the doorknob, but then turned back around. "I promise I won't tell anyone. I don't think Allison would like it too much, to be honest."

Thank the Gods, I thought. Wait, Allison wouldn't like it? What kind of relationship do they have? I thought they broke up. Why would Allison care? Why would Montana care? What did I just get myself into?

Ashton left, and I raced for Jaden's bike, needing an escape. I had no destination, only a journey to find answers, and the speed felt good. Faster and faster I pedaled, higher and higher into the mountains. I didn't want Montana to worry. I didn't want Allison to be mad. So why had I let it happen? And why had kissing two girls scared me? I had kissed thousands of Gods.

Why now? Why when I kissed two mortals—two mortal girls—did I start freaking out?

I reached the top of the mountain and dropped the bike near the big boulder. I was not done, though. My body kept pushing me, so I ran to the top of the boulder and leaped off the side of the mountain. I wished to fly away. The wind pressed against my stomach and arms as I greeted the fall. It was a hundred-foot drop and I landed hard on the balls of my feet. A pain shot up through my legs, but I ignored it and dashed up another trail, away from whatever it was. Fear? Or was I running *to* something?

I don't know how far or for how long I ran, but eventually I sprinted back up to the mountaintop, finally slowing down as I reached Jaden's bike. I took a seat on the giant rock, the pressure of my own thoughts building up again. Was this what an anxiety attack felt like? Rain sprinkled down onto my cheeks and arms. I stared at my skin that no longer glowed—my mortal-looking skin—and felt a sharp pain in my legs and back. Pain I had never experienced before. Was I becoming one of them? My head shot up to the sky, and I wished for the Gods to hear my thoughts. A couple drops of water landed on my cheeks.

They must be spitting at me. Or Persephone is crying for me. The rain continued to come down in soft sprinkles on my forehead and eyelids. I wiped it from my cheeks. It was the closest I would come to crying.

My phone vibrated loudly in my jacket pocket, and I lifted it out. My heart dropped. Was it from Montana?

"Hey Pei, let's go get breakfast. I'm starving!"

My heart lifted again, enabling me to breathe. It was only Jaden.

∞

I must have been starving. I had eaten my whole plate—and even some of Jaden's.

She stared at me like I was some kind of ravenous animal. "Last night was fun, huh?"

I looked at her, smiling. *What does she mean by that? Does she know what happened?*" Yeah, it was," I mumbled.

"Did Ashton end up spending the night?"

Was she asking or antagonizing me? "Yeah she did."

"In your bed?" She knew. I was done. She knew something had happened.

I nodded slowly.

"Okay, phew."

"Phew?"

120

"I thought you were talking to yourself. Good to know you were talking to someone!" she said, giggling. "I thought you were going crazy or having a bad dream. I was going to check on you, but I was too lazy to get out of bed."

I sighed, relieved. "Ha, yeah." I laughed uneasily. "I was talking to her for a long time."

"Yeah? About?" she asked eagerly. "About her ex and other things."

"Yeah?"

What? Did she want to know more? My heart began to pound faster. Harder. I needed to tell her the truth. She would be suspicious if I didn't. Maybe I could act like it didn't mean anything. "Ha! Yeah, and then we kissed!"

Jaden stopped chewing, letting out the biggest laugh. "You guys did? Oh man, that's awesome."

The restaurant got quiet . . . or was it the inside of my mind? "Wha— Why is that awesome?"

"I don't know. Just is. She's hot," she said nonchalantly, shrugging.

"I-It's not awesome," I muttered.

"What? You never kissed a girl before?"

I didn't answer. I stared at her secure smile and felt my own face fall.

"Are you all freaked out?" She reached over and grabbed my drink, taking a sip. "Well don't be. Everyone does it at some point in their life." She put my drink back and then smiled. "And if they haven't, then they probably have at least thought about doing it."

Her words were oddly reassuring. Why was I making such a big deal about it? Why was Montana making a big deal? I almost wanted to ask her. I reached for my phone and looked at the last text she'd sent me last night.

"Hey, are you awake?"

Chapter 23

One Last Time

Another month passed. Montana was avoiding me—again—and her absence had left me empty inside. I wondered how long she would keep her disappearing act up and hated how I constantly worried about her. My mind began to fill up with thoughts of her instead of my studies. And all my teachers had assigned twenty-page papers, so with five classes, my time was limited. I needed my focus back.

I couldn't study at home anymore—Britta's obnoxious emotions were affecting me. It felt like I was going crazy with everything going on: the confusing pressure on my chest, kissing girls, starting to feel emotions, my skin not glowing anymore, finals approaching, and now Britta. There was too much to get a handle on.

I headed to the library with all my books stacked in my arms. My phone vibrated in my back pocket, so I stopped walking, shifted the books to one side to free up a hand, and pulled it out. I tried to steady the books as they teetered side to side, but the tower fell to the ground. I stood there staring at them, hoping Hades would ignite them.

It wasn't a text from Montana as I had hoped. My inbox used to be filled with her texts, but now they were replaced by Ashton's. I was thankful for her. Not talking to Montana had slit me open, and the wound grew bigger each day she didn't talk to me. But Ashton filled in the cut somewhat. We talked about everything except that night and the strange paranoid way Montana had reacted. Ashton had so many great stories about her and Allison and what they had been through—what she'd had to face, what Allison had had to face, and the beautiful aftermath of getting through it all together.

I clicked to open the text.

We're going out tonight! Everyone! I already talked to Tawny, Sade, and Allison. They're down. And you know Jaden and Diane will be too. Can't wait to see you! ;)

I smiled and then reread the text. My smile fell when I didn't see the one name I wanted to see most. There was only one week left until summer, and then it would be three months before I would see her again. My body shook at the thought. I didn't know why I cared so much, especially since one week of school also meant one week until I was back home in the Heavens with my family and friends.

I walked into the library and immediately wanted to run back out. What I had dreaded was finally here. The tortured pain of anxiety twisted against my body and inside my head, aching as I walked by each stressed student.

The pain hit me like a huge fan on full blast and got more powerful as I walked deeper into the crowded library, looking at students 'faces as I passed. It was strange—although it felt like their minds were ready to explode from all the pressure, they looked completely composed on the surface. Each student was straight-faced, showing no hint of pain or worry, yet my ears rang with their loud emotions.

Since I had been around mortals more, I had come to realize that they had a power of their own: the ability to show no emotion on the outside when their insides were screaming. They were stronger than I had realized. We Deities underestimated them way too much. One day our presumptions would backfire on us.

I headed quickly to the back of the library—away from the emotional turbulence, where the ringing mercifully started to subside. I turned the corner at the last row of bookcases, and my textbooks fell from my hands. I must have startled her just as much as she had me, because Montana jumped and moved away at an unreal speed. *She is avoiding me.* I had to blink the thought from my mind. I needed to leave. I turned around and quickly walked to one of the quiet study rooms in a separate part of the library.

My heart felt like it was crawling up my throat. I kept swallowing, trying to push it back down, but my throat only felt more clogged. Why would she be avoiding me? It hurt so badly seeing her run from me. But why did I care so much? I needed to compose myself. Having to compose my emotions was another change I resented. Tonight is going to be a good night, I kept repeating to myself.

∞

Jaden, Diane, and I left the house a little after nine. We picked a booth near the bar and settled there to wait for the rest of the girls. Ashton walked in and got the biggest smile on her face when she saw me. She continued past our booth to the corner of the bar but turned her head and winked at me.

I saw Jaden's mouth open, but what she said was drowned out suddenly by what I felt from Ashton. Her body tensed up a thousand times greater than any human I had ever felt, to the point where I thought she was going to explode. I turned to see what was happening. She was glaring past me, toward the entrance.

Montana was five feet away from me, walking toward our booth with Tawny, Sade, Allison, and a couple other girls. What happened next, I will never forget. She glared at me, and I wanted to disappear. Her eyes screamed at me—cursing and crying. I felt my heart skip and land with a pound, and then pick up again, faster and faster. I reached for my chest like it was exposed. It felt like she wanted to throw me into the wall, grab me and hold me close, shove me as far away as she could, and then wrap her arms around me again and kiss me. Her tortured grin confirmed the twisted thought process. I turned from her and found Sade's eyes. She felt easy and light—she just wanted to have a good time. And so did I.

The rest of the girls felt the same way, too. Except Ashton. I could feel the emotion burning inside her. It was going to be an interesting night.

Montana and the other girls went to the dance floor, and I stayed at the table by myself, enjoying the neon lights reflecting off the glossy tabletop. I stared at the lit candle on the table. The wax was almost gone, but the flame flickered on, waving in the drafty air.

Allison took a seat in front of me.

"Hey, Petra." Her words were easy, but her grin was curious.

I nodded and smiled. Her grin grew almost too big for her face and her voice rose in volume. "You know, we weren't going to come tonight."

My head was dancing to the beat of the music, but I stopped once I caught her implication. "Why was that?"

She bobbed her head to the rhythm nonchalantly, and then smiled at me like that was exactly the question she wanted me to ask. "Because Taylor didn't want to come."

I had thought so. "Why didn't she want to come?" I knew the answer, but I asked to see if it was as obvious to others.

She leaned back into her seat and relaxed her head on the cushion. "I don't know." She looked at me intensely. "Maybe because she heard you were coming."

I didn't get what the big deal was, but the tension I felt from Ashton when she stared at Montana did not seem small.

I stared through Allison to the red wall behind her.

"She thinks we're getting in the way." She spun her empty glass with her fingers as she waited for my reply.

"Getting in the way?"

She leaned on the table and stared into my eyes. I stared right back, and for the first time, I saw the patterns in them—they were not just caramel, but swirled with drips of honey. They looked good enough to eat. She opened her mouth to speak, and I shifted my gaze away so I could pay attention to her words.

"Getting in the way of her being with you."

I laughed for what seemed like a long time. Montana had been avoiding me for a month—I was sure she wanted just the opposite. I got myself under control and noticed Allison wore a somber face.

"Here she comes," she warned.

When I smelled her perfume behind me, my heartbeat immediately halted. I wanted to close my eyes, but they did not obey, so I stared down at the candle. She sat down next to me and smiled, but it was not her that was doing it. Alcohol was providing the smile. I stared at the empty glass in her hand and then back up to her glassy eyes. She looked beautiful when flushed. I felt a smile coming from Allison as she looked at us. I sensed all the other girls in good spirits. They surrounded the table, laughing obnoxiously with each other.

The bar was about to close, and we were acting as if it had just opened. All the girls were reminiscing and taking pictures to remember their last night at the bar. I sat back in the booth as I lived the moment with them, feeling all the great times they'd had with each other. Montana, Jaden, Diane, and I were the only ones returning next year.

I was heading toward Jaden's car when I felt soft fingers against the palm of my hand and looked up to see Montana giving me a worried look. I allowed her to lead me.

Her jeep was over capacity with all of us piled in. I don't know how we fit, but we did. After dropping the other girls off, we finally parked at Montana's and ran quickly inside to beat the cold. I slumped on the couch, and Allison sat by my side. Sade went directly to the kitchen to prepare something, and Tawny grabbed a bag of chips and lay down on the couch next to us. Montana retired to her room. I watched to see if she would turn to look at me.

I felt Allison's curiosity crawling up my neck, so I turned to look at her. She nodded. Her curiosity was for my benefit—she wanted me to be curious. And I was. I got up at her unspoken demand and headed toward Montana's bedroom.

She was already in bed. I made my way to the edge of her bed and thought about saying something, but then the questions would just pour out: *Why were you avoiding me? Why have you left me alone?*
"Hey?" was all I could get out.

"Hey. Are you staying here tonight?" she asked, sounding a bit worried.

"No, I'm going to walk back home. I just wanted to say goodnight."

She looked up at me and reached for my arm, wrapping her delicate hands around my wrist. "Stay here," she said softly.

idea."

I could not. I should not. But why not? "I don't think that's a good

She loosened her grip on my wrist, but then tightened it again. "Why?" Why? Why, Petra? Why isn't it a good idea? Friends have slumber parties all the time. But a friend wouldn't have an urge, a certain urge . . . "I'm afraid I'll kiss you again." I hoped I had whispered it just softly enough that she couldn't hear me, but she did. I felt her hand loosen around my wrist. *I scared her,* I thought, and began hyperventilating, choking as I swallowed air.

What she did next was totally unexpected. She got out from under the covers and moved off her bed. I backed out of the way. She walked across the room and pressed a button on her stereo. A song began to play, and I began to smile. It was the song I had told her about—my favorite song. She hopped back into bed and looked at me.

I wanted to kiss her then, while the violins played. I leaned over her—not to her lips, but to her cheek. She would give me that, hopefully. I gently placed my lips against her satin skin. I wanted to hold them there for as long as she would let me, but I pulled away, dragging my bottom lip across her cheek, and as I stepped back to avoid her lips, she started moving her head to the perfect angle, lifting her head from the pillow, reaching for me—and slowly met my lips. I felt my chest close, and I became complete—whole.

We let go of each other gently, and I looked down at her smiling face, at her long hair sprawled over the pillow. She picked up another pillow stashed on the side of her bed, placed it next to her, and patted it, beckoning me to lay with her. I tried to sense something—anything—in that smile, but there was nothing, of course. I climbed into bed and lay my head down next to her, pulling the covers over me. My feet skimmed down her legs, and I felt her become rigid with that sudden touch. I remained motionless, staring at the blank ceiling, thinking, *if only I could sense one thing from her.* She scooted closer to the edge of her bed, turning her body away from me once again, and fell asleep.

Chapter 24

Last Days of School

The beast roared loudly in my face as its spit flew everywhere. My hair was soaked in its saliva, and I cried out in fear and disgust. Its gigantic face was masked in black, which I was thankful for because even the beast's silhouette was hideous. In the distance, past the beast's oversized head, was a familiar bright light and blurry shadow figure. I struggled to get a better look, but the beast's head was six times the size of mine. It had thick chunks of hair spiked messily around it, followed by a long, braided ponytail growing from the back and hanging down its body, which looked a lot like a lion's. Was I in Hades? I must be. I found myself crying. Why was I crying? I looked down at how weak I looked without my glowing skin and wiped away my tears as I stared into the beast's giant mouth. I did not budge—my feet were planted as I listened to the beast's angry cries.

I dove out of the dream and back into the morning sun. Had I been talking in my sleep? I looked down at Montana. Still asleep. *Good.* I hopped out of bed, grabbed my shoes, and left the room. Allison and Sade were passed out on the couches. I was careful not to wake them because I didn't want them to know I had stayed the night.

I went out the front door and started running home. Microscopic knives hit my face as I ran into the freezing wind. May was not supposed to be this cold. Where was Persephone? I kept running until I reached my house, but stopped right before the front door to turn and look at the sky. I watched the colors transform into a warm fire, blues and purples forming a cooling layer beneath the red and orange morning sky. And as I followed the colors with my eyes, watching them twist with the clouds, a disheartening thought entered my mind: *She will try to avoid me again.* And I was sadly right.

That day was déjà vu—a repeat of the first time Montana and I had kissed. She didn't speak to me, nor try contacting me in any way. What had I done now? Why did she hate me so much?

There was a time when I felt nothing—when I felt everyone else's emotions and just had to pretend I understood them. And then a time came when I began to feel my own. But still nothing from her. She was empty to me.

∞

On Sade and Tawny's graduation day, Jaden, Britta, and I showed up late. We were about to go around the fence behind the graduates, but then I spotted Montana with Ashton. They were laughing together—the opposite of the last time I'd seen them together, when they'd avoided each other.

Ashton spotted me and whispered something in Montana's ear. Ashton met my eyes, squinting, and gave me a look like I didn't belong. It was the weirdest reaction I had yet seen from her. Montana finally glanced toward me, but then quickly looked away. What the heck was going on?

I moved toward Ashton, but stopped abruptly in my tracks when I spotted Nick behind them. Surprisingly, they did not notice him or his glow. What was he doing here? I only took one step before I ran smack into his sandals. "Petra, don't," he said. He was right in my face.

That alone was a

Warning

"What?" I waited for his furious expression to subside into something less threatening, but it did not. "Why?"

"Just leave it alone, okay?" he said flatly. He glared at me a bit longer without saying a word, and then slowly turned to rejoin Ashton and Montana.

The rest of the graduation ceremony was a blur. That night, however, was one I would never forget.

I came home from running errands late. Very late. I had to return to the Heavens early the next day, and I still had to pack my things. I rushed through the front door and headed toward my room, but something pretty wrapped in tinsel on the couch caught my eye. The card taped to the tinsel read "Britta" in big red letters. On the bottom it said, "From Taylor Letto."

"Cute, huh?" I turned to find Britta standing next to me wearing an overzealous grin. "She dropped it off before saying goodbye."

"She left?" My voice rose.
She gave me a weird look, and right after, I felt her curiosity explode inside me.

"She's leaving at four tomorrow morning, so she wanted to come over and say goodbye—to me."

"Cool," I muttered, then walked into my room and shut the door.

I dove into my covers. My forehead felt permanently creased—I had been frowning for a very long time. Why was I angry? The pressure on my chest had returned, more intense than usual. I wanted it to leave. I wanted her to leave. She annoyed me, ignored me—and she had made me this way.

I licked the single tear clinging to my lip. And I cry because of her.

Another tear slid down the side of my nose and onto my cheek. I closed my eyes, wishing to be back on my pretend island where I did not hurt and did not cry. I prayed to the Gods for my old life back—I wanted to be how I was before I knew her. I'd had enough of this crying and feeling.

I flung the covers off, breaking the chains that held my body, and headed toward the front door. I walked all the way to campus, up her walkway, up the stairs to her door, and knocked. Sade answered.

"Hey Petra, what's up?"

"Can you get Taylor for me?" I asked, not missing a beat.

I waited only a few minutes before she appeared. Without saying a word, I grabbed her hand and led her down the stairs and down the walkway. Once I thought we had reached a distance far enough from her place, I stopped. She stepped in front of me. I wondered if she would be able to see where my tears had fallen, so I focused my eyes on the ground to hide my face.

"What do you want, Petra?" she asked condescendingly.

With my hand, I pushed back the sudden ball of pressure in my chest—that one hurt me. I could barely speak. "I–I wanted to say goodbye. You weren't going to."

Warily, I waited for her response. The silence floated around us both for a while.
"I'm sorry," she said, and I felt something then. "I just couldn't." It was her shield. Had I made a dent?
"Couldn't?" It came out a whimper. I must have sounded pathetic.

"I couldn't say goodbye," she whispered.

"You were going to leave me . . . without a goodbye?" I was whimpering again.
Another long pause. I lifted my head for one last look at her eyes. With our track record, this might be the last time I would ever see them. They glistened in the light from the streetlamps, and for a second, it looked as if she was about to cry.

She leaned forward, wrapping her arms around me, and I held her gently as she gripped me tightly. She locked her hands into place behind me and didn't let go, holding me as if I was leaving for war and this would be the last time she would ever see me.

She finally let go and leaned back, stopping when her face was right in front of mine. I felt my heart pound through my chest. My pulse vibrated so strongly throughout my body that I was sure she could feel it. The rushing blood warmed me instantly. I felt Montana's heart as well, beating the same beats as mine. The cadence of her breathing matched mine. We were one and the same at that moment in time. I dove into her whole being while standing still; I was inside her, and I never wanted to let go of this moment.

But her lips did not continue their course toward mine. Instead, she pulled back and looked at me.

"Thank you," she said. And then she spun around and walked back to her townhouse, leaving me in a trance, totally confused and not understanding what had just happened.

I walked back home with the biggest smile on my face. My heart was racing, and in a way I felt unafraid. I didn't know what was happening to me, but I knew it was something different, something special.

I was not paying attention, and soon was almost home. Before I reached my driveway, I heard my name being screamed. I looked up. Dion and were Apria running towards me, and they felt horrified.

"Petra!" Apria yelled again. Before taking any more steps, they both sped up ten times faster than the average mortal and were in front of me within a blink of an eye.

"Petra, its John." I heard Apria's voice before I felt her grab my shoulders. "They found John!"

"He's in the Underworld, Petra." Dion's voice shook with horror. "He's gone to ask Hades now!"

My smile quickly vanished. I could still hear them screaming, and yet it felt muted by my thoughts, as if my body had numbed itself from the news and I could not comprehend the severity of their words. I felt her lips suddenly. And then I fell back onto the pillow. I touched her legs and drifted off to sleep. I saw her eyes and felt warm. Her eyes turned gold, and her face morphed into John's. His face carried me back to reality.

Suddenly their voices unmuted. And in between their shouts, I managed to say, "I must get him."

Dion's bronze eyes and Apria's sapphire ones both regarded me with worry, afraid of

what they knew I had to do, what I was going to say. And sure enough, I said it. "We need to go to the Underworld."

130

Chapter 25

The Underworld

Blood was the river, and the heart was its source. In an endless cycle, the heart gives blood away and takes it back. That was the Underworld. Five great rivers flowed there. Styx River was the main artery, and it separated into four other rivers, each leading into different realms. Each river had its own purpose and power.

Styx connected the physical world on Earth to the spiritual world.

It was the river of immortality. One sip of its waters, and you would live forever.

Phlegethon was the burning stream to the south, flowing to Mt. Tartarus.

Acheron, the river of pain, flowed to the west. Hades 'ferryman, Charon, used Acheron to transport dead souls into the Underworld, where they were purified by fire until they were forever cleansed and freed from pain.

Cocytus, the wailing river, flowed to the east. The river cried with those whose souls could not be purified and was said to be the river that made wolves howl at night.

And lastly, there was Lethe, the river of forgetfulness and concealment, flowing to the north. This river was for moral mortals who deserved to live again. One sip from Lethe's waters would make them forget the life they'd had and be reborn with a new one. It was a restart button, but the catch was that they were not allowed to remember anything from before.

Finding the Underworld was challenging for both mortals and Gods. It was the heart, and yet the hardest portal to reach. Once you spotted Styx, the artery could lead you there, but it was often found in the most unlikely places.

Dion, Apria, and I dove into the Red Sea's waters, swimming vigorously against the current. Once we saw where land began, we swam beneath it until the current changed, pushing us further under. Without a breathing apparatus, no humans could survive—the pressure from the depths alone would crush them. Darkness surrounded us, but Dion and Apria's Deity glow served as our lantern. The current took us deeper underneath the landmass until we came to an underwater cave. Once we were inside, the cave dried, and before us appeared the Styx River.

Standing at the head of the river was the God Charon, Hades 'ferryman. He wore gold-plated armor over a large chest, and a helmet with bull's horns curved above his head and two bloodred gems between them, serving as the bull's eyes. Charon himself had dark eyes, but a thin circle of gold outlined each black pupil. His mouth was large, with oversized lips, but he stood mute, saying nothing. He stretched out his arm, palm upturned.

Any courageous mortal who overcame the obstacles to get to the Styx River would be greeted by Charon. The mortal would then be required to give him two coins. These coins were not a payment. Rather, Charon would turn the coins into gold and place them on the mortal's eyes in order to shield them from the fire and intensity of the river. Without the coins, mortals would be petrified. For Gods, however, no coins were needed.

One at a time, Charon took our hands and helped us onto the boat. We remained quiet as he allowed the vessel to drift upstream.

The Styx was unlike any river I had ever seen before. It was very wide and continued as far as the eye could see. It had no bends or falls, no current or grade. It was as if we sailed on a massive conveyer belt. I peered over the edge to see the river up close—until Charon hit me with his hooked staff.

Black as onyx and thick as tar, it did not look like a river at all. Off in the distance on either side of Styx's banks were bright red petrified trees. Their red trunks did not sprout from the ground, for there was no ground that I could see. Instead, their roots dangled freely, growing everywhere and entangling with those of neighboring trees. Off in the distance, beyond the red trees, a blazing sky of red, orange, and yellow mimicked the Heavens ' sunset but did not share its warmth. Upon reaching land again, the boat collided with the dock with a big thud. We spotted a large gate in the distance, tall as a mountain and shiny black as if constructed from obsidian. We were nearly thirty feet away, and we still had to crane our necks to take in its full height. With great trepidation, we stepped onto the dock, waved Charon on, and trekked toward the gate. It began opening slowly when we were halfway there, seemingly anticipating our arrival. We hesitated before going through. I looked at Apria and Dion and saw a hint of fear on their faces. I was the first one to step through the gates, wearing John's name as a shield, and using my love for him as my courage.

It was cold, but I did not feel cold. I did not sense death or despair or suffering. I did not sense anything. It was dark, and the air was still. I would have thought I was floating if I had not felt the rocky ground beneath me. As I walked, I listened, but I heard nothing. It was completely quiet. Everything was quiet. And I liked it.

But suddenly the air turned foul—old and moldy, as if we stood in a field of fungus. A light breached the opaque ceiling and we saw we were standing in the dust of, sure enough, weeds and fungus. The light hid itself in a dark vortex above us, smearing some of its illumination across the mocking sky. And then, in a flash, I began sensing something warm. From Apria and Dion's glow, we saw that we stood near a stream, which grew in width further down. On the other side of the stream, the terrain was prettier, with the starts of green grass growing. We walked closer, peering down at it. I somehow knew that it was the River Lethe. It was a small stream, no more than seven feet wide.

"Let's jump it," I suggested. The others nodded their heads.

We moved back from the stream, giving ourselves enough space to build up momentum, and then began running. I leaped over the stream, my arms flailing above me, and landed on the opposite side.

Instead of grass, I was confronted by an empty darkness. I could still feel the warmth—and this time it was a little stronger—but I was still unclear as to what it was. That warmth was the only thing I could sense in the darkness around me.

Dion and Apria's glow had vanished, and I could not see them anywhere. I wasn't even sure they were even with me now.

"Apria? Dion? Are you there?" I called. My voice did not echo or carry at all in the darkness. It sounded flat and muffled, like I was shouting from a closed-up box. They did not answer, so I decided to press onward toward the warmth.

After two steps, I felt something scratch my back, but when I turned around, I saw only darkness. I shrugged and began walking again, but then something scratched me a second time. This time, it was slow, as if a finger dragged its nail down my neck. Then suddenly, I felt five tracks down my spine. The fingers tightened, digging sharp nails into my skin. Another hand grabbed my shoulder, pulling me back, another encircled my wrist, and another grasped my ankle. Soon, nearly a dozen hands snatched at my limbs, pulling me away from the warmth I sensed.

I could not see to whom the hands belonged, and the darkness began playing with my imagination. I did my best to ignore what was happening and continue my march towards the warmth. The hands were strong, though. One reached for my foot as I took a step, tripping me. I fell to the cold ground and scrambled to pick myself back up.

Just keep going Petra. Ignore it and go.

I dragged my feet with each step, pulling the hands from my body as I proceeded. The nails dug deeper, scratching even harder as I tried to move away. I could feel my skin breaking and bleeding, and then trying to repair itself before the next scratch.

Now the ground was beginning to soften. My feet began to sink as I tried to tear away from the menacing claws. A hand grabbed my neck and I took one gigantic step forward, expending so much effort that I thought I must have torn the unseen limb from its socket. The hand fell off and back into the darkness. One more step, and I ran into something hard. A wall. Or what seemed to be—it was still pitch black, and I couldn't tell. I must have reached the end of the abyss, but I could still feel the warm force pulling me. I turned around to face where I thought the hands had been coming from, but I saw only blackness. My back was against the wall, and I slid down to the soggy ground. I had no idea what I should do, and so I called out for my friends.

"Dion!" I shouted "Apria?"

No answer. I faced the wall and slammed my fists against it once, and then again, hoping it would budge.

I stopped to see if I could still sense the force, and I could. I could still feel its warmth. It was calling for me, beckoning me. Again, I slammed my fists against the wall, harder this time. Again and again and again.

No sound, not even the echo of my pounding. I slouched back down to the ground. And then it hit me. A weight fell over my shoulders and chest and sent shivers across my body. My shield began to fall, and my courage began to crumble as the dark force started its crawl. Up my chest, slithering around my neck, finally fighting off the last bit of courage I had. The dark force dove into my head. Fear. I was afraid.

The fear tingled through my fingers and up my arm, making the hairs stand up. I had goosebumps all over—from my spine to my neck to the top of my head. My eyes stung and burned, and my nose tingled.   Suddenly, my eyes began to swell up. I had felt this before but didn't know its meaning until finally tears started to fall from my eyes. I want more than anything to save John.

The tears running down my cheeks were my final realization that I was changing and had softened into a mortal. Another tear fell from my cheek, and I caught it in the palm of my hand. I didn't know whether I liked what was happening to me or not, but I wanted to see the tear I was holding.

I stared down into the blackness to where my hand should be, and began wishing, praying . . . hoping. The fear devoured my courage but did not destroy it. I felt it trying to revive and push through the dark force.

Suddenly, a single white dot formed in my hand and I realized it was a speck of light, reflecting from the tear I was holding.

I watched as the reflection grew larger and larger, until I was able to see my hand and then my arm. The light was coming from a small slit on the black wall, which opened wider until a rectangular door formed, illuminated by the light. I wiped the tear off my palm and walked through the door.

The white surrounding me was extremely bright. I covered my eyes as they tried to adjust.

"Pei!" I heard a voice say.

"Petra!" another one called.

I uncovered my eyes in time to see Apria and Dion wrapping their arms around me. I looked at myself and noticed my clothes were intact—they had not been shredded by the clawing hands like I'd thought.

"Petra! Where did you go?" Apria cried.

"One moment we were crossing the Acheron, and the next thing I knew, you were gone," said Dion.

I backed away from their hugs. "Acheron River?" I asked. "No, we crossed the river of Lethe."

Their worry was immediately evident.

"Lethe?" Apria asked, sounding startled.

"Why would we cross Lethe?" Dion asked right after.

I shook my head at his question. "We crossed the Styx together, didn't we?"

"Yes," Apria said, sounding annoyed. "We boarded Charon's boat, entered the gates, and then we crossed—"

"Lethe. We crossed Lethe."

"No—Acheron," Apria argued. "Petra, why Lethe? What's going on with you?"

I looked at the ground and saw a ring forming. I realized I was the one creating it as I walked in circles. "You guys." I stopped walking to look at them. "I don't remember crossing Acheron. I only remember crossing Lethe."

"Where did you end up?" Apria asked, her voice softer than before.

"I was somewhere dark. Really dark. I had no clue where I was. But I felt something warm, so I kept walking toward it. Hands were grabbing me all over. And then I hit a wall. I was banging and banging—"

"I think Hades led her there, Apria," Dion whispered.

"Led me there for what?"

I needed to sit down. I felt that same fear begin to sit on my chest again. I staggered back and kneeled on the white floor, gasping for air.

Apria rushed to my side and kneeled next to me.

"Apria, what is Dion talking about?"

Her gentle fingers gripped my shoulder. I tried focusing on her touch instead of the heavy weight on my chest. My lungs sought more air, but I could not seem to get enough to fill them.

"Petra, relax," Apria soothed. "I need you to look at me. You need to relax. Look at me."

My lungs felt as if they were filling with water. My breathing was shallow. I realized she was right. I needed to relax. Gasping, I looked up at her. Her sapphire eyes glowed brighter. The white room reflected off her pupils, casting a light blue halo in the center of them.

"Petra, I need you to listen to me

carefully," I heard her say. I nodded, but was mesmerized by the halo in her eyes.

"Laws are enforced when Deities come to Hades 'Underworld. Certain laws need to be abided or else." She paused. "And one of those laws states no one can drink from any river without Hades 'permission." She paused again. "Did you drink from Lethe?"

I thought it was a trick question, for if I did drink from Lethe, I would not remember having done so. I shook my head. "From what I can remember, I did not drink anything."

"Okay. Have you ever been to the Underworld before?"

Her questions were getting absurd. The Underworld was not a theme park you took your family to. It was a place most Gods and Goddesses stayed far away from.

"No. I don't get why you're asking me these stupid questions, Apria."

I looked between them, saw Dion's face contort, and sensed his solemnity before he spoke.

"Pei, you must have been here before, and you somehow drank from the river. Hades had you come back to finish crossing Lethe—to complete the process of your incarceration." He paused and shot Apria a look. "Or someone gave you Lethe's river water to drink without Hades 'permission.

Either way, Pei, you being brought to the river today means something." He looked at Apria again.

I could sense him conjuring up another heavy thought to burden me with, but I did not want to hear it. I got up and walked away from Dion's ridiculous misconceptions.

To me, this was all unlikely. Incarceration? Complete the process? Led here for a reason? Had I been dead before? Was I punished before? Had I been here before? All these thoughts birthed simultaneously in my mind, and my head began to pound.

"Petra, wait!" I heard Apria shout, but I kept walking into the bright lights that came from everywhere. I didn't know where I was going, but I knew I needed to be far away from them.

"Pei, what about John!" Dion shouted.

I stopped. John! I turned back toward them and nodded. "We'll discuss this later."

∞

We reached a cave. It was a typical cave—wet, cold, and dark.

All around the cave—against the walls, hanging from the jagged ceiling, climbing up the rocky sides—were disgustingly tall, grey, starving bodies. Perhaps the hands attacking me in the black room belonged to them.

In front of us, a decrepit bridge was suspended twenty feet above the Cocytus River. Anyone could identify the Cocytus: dead bodies rippled on the surface of the water, reaching out and crying for air. A wave of cries penetrated the cave walls, echoing back down into the waters until another wave came to take its place.

I was thankful we had the bridge to cross over instead of having to use the rocky plateaus on the sides. One being suddenly jumped from the ceiling and onto the bridge, landing on the railing next to Dion. We froze. It looked even more hideous up close. Its face appeared to be falling off the bone, and its skin was taut against its ribs and spine.

We scooted past the creature, shuffling our feet, keeping an eye on it lest it attack. We finally put distance between us, but still the creature sat staring at us with its intense, blackened eyes. We had almost reached the end of the bridge. I turned around for one last look and saw that all of the creatures had gathered together, forming a huge barrier that cut us off from where we had just come.

The creatures were intimidating as they watched us, waiting for us to do something. One of them—the one closest to us—moved. It lifted an elongated, grey hand to another creature's ear, and it said something.

Apria grabbed my hand as I saw a finger pointing past her and at me. It was usually Apria who got all the stares. But this time, it was me they were pointing at, as if they knew who I was.

As Apria held onto my hand, I felt her fear. I reached out for Dion's hand and held it, too, feeling his confusion and excitement. I closed my eyes and could feel my courage, still driving me to John.

138

We stepped off the bridge onto thick, mushy ground. That was when I felt the warmth again, pulling me toward it. Stronger now…wanting me.

It vibrated loudly through my body and pulled me forward as if a string connected me to it from my heart.

My feet sank in the mushy ground, and I fell forward, squishing my hands into the soft earth. I began to crawl up the sticky hill, laboring to pull my hands and feet up, and then plunge them back into the tar-like substance. And then I felt the warmth on my skin, as if a sun had risen from the horizon. I looked up and saw John on a rocky platform a couple of feet from me. His back was to us, and he was kneeling. His head hung, and his arms were pinned behind his back, as if he were a prisoner.

I lifted my hand from the mush and tried to sprint toward him with all my power, but the tar made it too much of a challenge. I could not gain any speed. My feet remained stuck to the ground. Instead of running, I had to pull my feet out one at a time.

After what felt like an eternity, I finally stepped onto the rocky platform, climbed up to John, and slid in front of him, grabbing his face in desperation.

"John! John!" His face was lifeless and pallid, and his eyes were glazed. He gave no response to my cries. I glanced around him and saw the broken bow and arrows surrounding him. I grabbed his shoulders and shook him violently. Still no response. No sign of life. My fingers weakened. No life. Nothing.

"John?" I cried. Was he dead? Was I too late? "John, can you hear me?" I screamed.

I did not think his soul inhabited his body, but I couldn't believe it—I kept staring at his face, hoping to see any flinch in his frozen gaze. And then I looked past him and saw Apria and Dion working to move through the sticky, mushy flooring—struggling horribly.

I had failed John. I had come too late. It wasn't fair. . . I wanted him back. I wanted my brother back.

My hands felt weak as they slipped off his shoulders. What was I to do now?

Suddenly, my nose began to tingle. And quick as a flash of light, I started feeling it all over my body. My chest began its hard pounding. My body heated up as angry blood flowed through my veins. My stomach twisted up into my throat. My eyes became damp, and I put my hands to my face. I was back in the dark room, feeling the same thing. . . fear.

A single tear passed through my cupped hands. I felt it stream down my wrist, down to my elbow, and delicately leave my body, dripping onto the rocky platform. I removed my hands from my eyes and stared at the broken bow and arrows. The broken arrows represented my brother's broken heart. . . and now mine, as I felt I had lost him forever.

With that realization, more tears began to flow, and before I knew it, now it was I who was sobbing uncontrollably, just as I had seen John do at the cliff of Point Dume. A tear fell every second, unleashing everything I felt at that moment—anger that I was too late, frustration that I had failed, and devastation that I had lost him.

I kept my head down and watched the tears drip into my hands. Then I closed my eyes and imagined I was on my island again—back to my paradise with my friends and family. I could feel John then. I could see his goofy smile, hear his silly laugh, and feel his artistic hands holding mine. It felt real, like everything was okay.

Everything was okay. I allowed those words to echo in my head.

Hearing them over and over felt like a breath of love.

John's hands felt so tangible in mine—too tangible. I opened my eyes and looked down to see actual hands holding mine. I looked up and found myself staring into John's warm, golden eyes.

"John!" I screamed.

He let go of my hands and wrapped his arms around me. I closed my eyes tight. Was I dreaming? I opened my eyes again and saw that the broken arrows were now whole. I looked at John and watched tears roll from his eyes— eyes that were now full of life.

Dion and Apria finally arrived on the platform. They had not seen me crying. They had not seen anything. All they saw was John holding me and smiling. I looked past them to where the grey creatures had been, but saw only an empty cave.

"Thank you, Pei," John whispered into my ear as he hugged me tighter.

I felt another tear slide down my cheek and onto his shoulder.

"For what?" I whispered back.

"For coming for me, again."

I closed my eyes again, squeezing out the last of my tears. I felt his love. And for the first time, I felt my love for him. Finally.

"I'm here now," he whispered again. He lifted up his head and grinned at me. "Let's go home."

Chapter 26

The Shack

I sat on the front porch swing, looking out over our orchards. The transparent ground also gave me a view of Earth below.

The day was calm, not too much heat radiating from the sun's close rays, and there was neither a drop of rain nor a hint of thunder from the gray clouds gathering above me. The air was still. Everything was still.

I never used to stare at Earth for so long and didn't know exactly why I was now. Pondering, I supposed. Thinking about Dion and Apria. Their request was heavy on my mind, but their concern was valid. Now that the problem had hit so close to home, it seemed like time was running out. If not for emotions, John wouldn't have been tempted to become one of Hades' permanent slaves, and Dion wouldn't have been branded, enabling the Elders to ban him from the Heavens. It was feelings and the inability to control them that had led to these outcomes.

But sharing one's gifts was a painful process. It was something like taking blood from a human, though rather than being drawn out through a needle, it was sucked through the skin.

Our gifts are energy—matter existing in each of us. If I shared mine with the other Deities, the energy would split and be divided among them. It was a process—not a long one, but a very painful one. But I was willing, now, to go through it for my kind.

I felt him coming before his hands grabbed my shoulders. Turning lazily around, I saw John's lively face and warm smile. He was so handsome with the sun's rays reflecting off his golden hair. Beyond him, the grey clouds had become white cotton balls, sporadically tossed by the breeze.

"Petra, how are you this morning?" His voice was just as soft as the clouds.

"I'm well, thank you." I didn't need to ask how he was—I could feel the happiness radiating from his skin.

"It's a brand-new day. A new start." He stood over me, head held high, chest out, and hands on his hips.

I laughed. "Okay there, superhero. What are you going to do with this brand- new start?"

He plopped down next to me with such enthusiasm he nearly detached the swing from its ropes. I had never seen him look so beautiful. He did look like a brand-new God, fresh out of the Styx. I shook my head and smiled again, glad that he was back.

"What?"

"I'm just glad I have you back."

He laughed at my sincerity and shook his head. "Petra! You are changing as well!"

I tried to stop the swing's rocking so I could look at him squarely in the eye, but his legs kept pumping away. Did he know? I gave up trying to halt the swing and hopped off, then immediately began looking through the glass beneath my feet. I admired the forests on the mountaintops and the sheet of fog hugging them—fields and fields of pine trees painted so beautifully, as far as the horizon.

"How was it down there?" John asked, his voice trailing away. "Any new prospects yet?"

His sense of intrigue immediately overwhelmed me, and I looked up to see his huge grin. I sat down on the porch steps in front of his dangling feet, which tapped my back lightly with each forward rock of the swing.

"This is different. This is a mortal school . . ."

He laughed at what he thought was my attempt at sarcasm. "Petra, mortal or immortal, no one has a chance with you." He paused, as if pondering, then added, "Only one came close though. . ."

There was a long silence, and in that silence, I could feel him wanting something from me. I turned around to face him. "Just ask, John."

He hesitated, grinning and studying my expression carefully.

"Whatever happened to you and Ricky?"

At the sound of his name, I envisioned Ricky's gentle fingertips on the back of my neck. His touch was softer than anything in this world. He had a painter's hands, delicately brushing his fingers around my body. There was a time he had opened my chest, but nothing beat inside. I could still feel his warm touch turn cold.

"I couldn't love him," I said softly.

"What if you could? Do you think you'd still love him?"

It was an odd question. And yet, I still pondered it. "I don't think so," I answered honestly.

"Oh," he said with a sigh. He stood, touched my arm, and began walking past me. I followed.

"John? What are we doing?"

"I want to show you something."

We continued walking, through the peach trees. I must have looked like a kid in a candy store, passing each tree in amazement. All the trees were full—each peach a beautiful red and pink hue and perfectly sized. I grabbed one and bit into it. The taste was of home, and every atom in me was rejuvenated instantly. I felt alive again.

I finished the peach and noticed we were deep in the fields, deeper than I had ever gone, and then suddenly, we stopped. Before us was a run-down wooden shack that looked as if it would topple over on us at any minute. I gave John a look that asked, "Explain this?" but all he did was smile and grab my arm once again, tugging me toward the piece of plywood that served as the door.

As we entered, I ducked my head, thinking the ceiling would be low, but it was much higher than expected—about two stories high. The building stretched back fifty yards on the inside. On either side of me, where I thought the walls would be only inches from my shoulders, they stretched away a good few yards.

My jaw dropped when I saw what hung on the walls. This appeared to be someone's secret collection. Beautiful, valuable art pieces hung side by side from one end to the other. Monet, Rembrandt, Renoir, Géricault,

Delacroix, Manet—paintings I had never seen before. Perched on short pillars in front of the walls were lekythos, olpes, and other pieces of ancient Greek pottery. Each one depicted a scene in beautiful red, white, and black paint.

We reached the back of the shack and stopped. Some of these pieces I had seen before. To the far left was the marble statue of Hercules and Diomedes carved by Vincenzo de 'Rossi. My father had looked so young then.

Next to the statue was the jug that depicted father taking the Palladium of Troy while looking back at Odysseus. I had seen one like it before, but that had been in the Elders 'hall on Mount Olympus. The jug in front of me now was bigger and much older.

As my eyes roamed across the wall, absorbing the art, they landed on my father's weapons displayed in a glass box. His sword had been forged by the most highly-skilled smith, who had engraved boar imagery on the blade, his spear, his round shield, and his golden cuirass. All of his weapons had been passed down from his father Tydeus and blessed by Athena.

Finally, I caught sight of something in the corner, something that stood out from everything else. I moved closer and smiled when I realized what it was: a carved wooden statue of Athena, the Great Olympian Goddess of Wisdom. It was nearly five feet tall but stood three feet higher on its stand.

Thick glass surrounded it, but I was sure that anyone would recognize it as the Palladium of Troy. I laughed and shook my head. Stories had been told on Earth about my father taking it as one of his spoils in the Trojan War, but no one had been able to prove it.

I giggled, imagining my father during that time—a great warrior, but a kid at heart. I imagined the excitement he and Odysseus must have felt after stealing the Palladium, and all the lies they'd had to tell in order to keep it.

My father's stories of the Trojan War would never grow old, no matter how many centuries passed. John nudged me, jarring me from my thoughts. I looked at him and he nodded to a piece of art in the corner. I looked from John to the corner and then walked over to the glowing red and orange piece of pottery.

Slowly, I moved my face closer to it—scanning it up and down. I had never seen it before, and I couldn't make out the faces of the two female characters. One of them held a myrtle wreath; myrtle was one of Aphrodite's many signs.

"John, who is the woman next to Aphrodite?" I asked, my eyes still fixed on the piece.

He didn't answer me, nor did I feel him in the room, so I looked up to see if he was still there. He had an inquisitive look on his face. "John?"

He was quiet for a very long time before finally answering. "Her name is Peitho."

"Peitho?"

He nodded. "Who is Peitho?"

"Peitho was the Goddess of Persuasion and Seduction," he said.

Immediately, questions began to form in my mind, and they all spilled out before I could hold them back. "How do you know this? Why does father have it? I have never heard of Peitho. Who is she? And why is she with Aphrodite?"

I expected John to tell me to relax, but all he did was laugh and say, "When I was really young, I found this room one day as I played in the fields. Every so often, I would sneak out of the house to come here and see what else Dad had added. The last thing he added was that pottery piece." He paused. "Dad still doesn't know I know about this place." He smiled proudly. "But I don't know why he has this piece. I find it odd, too. Not until recently did I find out who she was.

"She was the counterpart of Aphrodite, the persuader and seductress. Supposedly, Peitho and Aphrodite were best friends. They were said to be always together, like a tag team. Their powers went hand in hand—like cookie dough and ice cream. Irresistible. No God stood a chance." He frowned. "Just imagine two incredibly beautiful Goddesses who were already capable of capturing a God with their looks, but now they could trap him with the powers of seduction and love." He shook his head, and I felt him tremble at the thought. "Poor, poor Gods. Back then, the Heavens were easily swayed by love and all its power."

"Cookie dough and ice cream, huh?" I laughed.

"Anyway," he said, ignoring me, "the reason why I brought you here, Petra, is because you remind me of her. Peitho. She was Aphrodite's best friend, and yet no one's heard of her. She doesn't have an ancestry or a lover. She doesn't have a story." He paused and looked down at the floor pensively, assembling what he wanted to say. He finally looked back up at me, and I saw his eyes glistening. A single tear perched on the edge of his lid, ready to fall. I felt him holding it back.

"My question to you is: What will Petra Ambrosi's story be?" I swallowed a hard knot in my throat.

"You have always been the persuader, Petra," he continued. "Always the seducer, which tells me you're searching for something."

His words turned the viewing glass around and pushed the telescope inside myself. His tear had vanished, but I hadn't seen it fall.

"I—I don't get what you're saying."

"Let a story be told. Be remembered."

"I-I don't." I lost what I was about to say. John watched me, worried. "Why does everyone worry about me?" My voice came out soft and quiet . . . broken.

"Because you're not living," he finally said.

Then I saw that same tear on his eyelid, still deciding whether or not to fall. I couldn't get myself to look into his eyes, even though I thought I should. Finally lifting my head, I saw the pain in them, and regrettably, watched the tear fall.

I closed my eyes, for I did not want to watch any more of his tears. I didn't know what to say. Instead ,I kept my eyes tightly closed and bathed in what I was feeling. Love. My love for John was so strong, so powerful. It felt as if I had been sleeping and a bucket of cold water was thrown on me. I finally woke up, then.

I opened my eyes and looked back at Peitho. Thoughts of Montana roared to the forefront of my mind, and tears began to build in my eyes. It was happening again.

I slowly moved away from the art, and away from John. I couldn't let my tears show. I stepped out of the shack and back into the peach orchards. I walked without looking and found myself in the middle of one of the aisles, not knowing which way was home. I whirled around to see which direction I should try, but stopped when I felt an angry energy. Nick was coming down the aisle.

"Petra!"

Why was he angry? I didn't move, waiting to see what he would do. He lifted his arm and pointed at me. Instantly, I remembered my dream. It was really happening. I started to step toward him, but in a blink, he was right in front of me.

"I warned you, Petra," he said despondently. He hung his head. "Now you're going to have to go. And you need to go now before the Horai come."
"What is going on, Nick?" I shouted.

He raised his head and stared hard at me. "I have to kick you out, Petra—"

The words caught in my throat. "W-What? Why?"

He put his hand on my shoulder and looked at me despairingly. "Because, Petra, you have been seen committing Lambda acts. The Moirai have seen your fate!" His voice rose. "I told you that all Lambdas had been kicked out of the Heavens to await judgment. I warned you to watch your actions." He paused, and in that pause, I watched his energy shift from anger to disappointment in an instant. "But you still acted improperly, and now I am forced to ban you from the Heavens. You and all the Lambdas." He grabbed my arm. "And you should go now—before the Horai come."

"But my family," I squealed. "Can't I say goodbye?"

"No," he cried, and I could feel his remorse. "I'm so sorry."

"They'll wonder where I am! Why I'm not at home!" I shouted. This did not feel real. It couldn't be happening.

"Just tell them something—anything. Tell them you have a summer job.

A-And you have to live on Earth. Just give it through the summer. This will all blow over if you just forget. Let her forget you—and you must forget her, Petra!" He tugged at my hand, desperately trying to pull me away. "Just forget, Petra. That is what will save you."

He put his arm around me and brought me with him, leading me even deeper into the fields. As he led me away, my phone began to vibrate. I took it out of my pocket, and we both read the screen.

Petra, I'm so glad you came to say goodbye last night. I can't get the thought out of my head of how awful I would have felt if I'd left without seeing you. So, thank you. Please, don't forget me over the summer.

Greek Gods and Goddesses

Listed in alphabetical order

λ Achelois λ
The Moon Goddess who washed away pain.

λ Aphrodite λ
The Goddess of Sexuality, Love, and Beauty.

λ Apollo λ
The God of Truth, Prophecy, Art, Music, and Poetry. His twin sister is
Artemis.

λ Ares λ
The God of Warfare and Battle.

λ Artemis λ
The Goddess of Hunting and Fertility. Her twin brother is Apollo.

λ Asclepius λ
The God of Healing.

λ Athena λ
The Goddess of Wisdom, Skill, Justice, and Strategy.

λ Charon λ
Hades 'ferryman. He led souls from Earth into the Underworld.

λ Chronos λ
The God of Time and Years.

λ Cronus λ
The youngest of the twelve Titans. He overthrew his father Ouranos
and castrated him. His sons—Zeus, Hades, and Poseidon—then
overthrew him, and he was sent to
Tartarus to be punished forever.

λ Demeter λ
The Goddess of the Harvest.

λ Diomedes λ
A great warrior who fought with Achilles and Odysseus in the Trojan
War.
He was King of Argos before Athena made him immortal.

λ Dionysus λ
The God of Wine, Festivities, and Ecstasy.

λ Eris λ
The Goddess of Discord.

λ Eros λ
The God of Sexual Love. Also known by his Roman name, Cupid.

λ Gaia λ
The Titanide, the mother Earth. She was the first Goddess, along with
her husband, Ouranos.

λ Hades λ
The God of the Underworld and brother to Zeus and Hades.

λ Helios λ
The God of the Sun.

λ Hephaestus λ
The God of Volcanoes, Fire, Technology, and Blacksmiths.

λ Hera λ
The Goddess of Women and Marriage. She was the wife of Zeus.

λ Hermes λ
The Messenger God.

λ Hestia λ
The Goddess of Family. She was also the virgin Goddess.

λ The Horai λ

Also called the Hours, which means "the correct moment" in Greek mythology. They were the three half-sisters of the Moirai. Each one had a different gift—justice, law, and peace.

λ Medusa λ

A female monster in Greek mythology. If anyone were to stare directly at her they would turn into stone.

λ The Moirai λ

The three sisters called the "Agents of Destiny" in Greek mythology. They figuratively controlled the lives of every mortal and immortal.

λ Oceanus λ

The Titan of the Ocean. He was one of the twelve Titans.

λ Ouranos λ

The Titan of Air or Sky. He was the first Titan and husband to Gaia.

λ Peitho λ

The Goddess of Persuasion and Seduction. Related to Aphrodite.

λ Persephone λ

The Queen of the Underworld and Daughter of Demeter.

λ Poseidon λ

The God of the Sea and of Earthquakes and brother to Zeus and Hades.

λ Titans λ

The Titans were the former generations of strong Deities preceding the Olympians They were overthrown by Zeus and the Olympians in a ten-year war called the Titanomachy and became the new rulers of the cosmos.

λ Zeus λ

The God of the Heavens and Thunder. He was King of the Olympian Gods and Goddesses, brother to Poseidon and Hades, and husband to Hera.

Aphrodite's Sister Collection

Aphrodite's Sister: The Goddess of Emotion (Book 1)

Aphrodite's Sister: The Angel (Book 2)

Aphrodite's Sister: The Hidden One (Book 3)

Lightning Source UK Ltd.
Milton Keynes UK
UKHW012046310123
416284UK00020B/140/J